Corn Crusaders MC

(South Coast Brothers #2)

Kacey Hamford

TO VICKY

LOVELY TO MEET YOU.

K. Hamford

Text copyright © 2015

Kacey Hamford

Table Of Contents

Acknowledgements

First of all I would like to thank my amazing partner for supporting me in my adventure of becoming a writer. For all of the late night and early mornings that I had to get up and write the story that just wouldn't let me sleep.

I'd like to thank and mention Lucii, my PA, editor, beta reader and most importantly my friend. She keeps me motivated and on the right track.

Stephanie from SP Cover Design, for this amazing cover.

Kathleen, Laura, Claire, Emma, Titian and Natalie who are my number one fans. For their great support, advice and encouragement.

Stef, who helped me write this amazing synopsis and helped with the content material.

Bonnie, who helped me out greatly in this book. Without her I wouldn't have had such detail and the true way a biker club works.

My street team, Kacey's Kick Ass Crew. Without all of your support in buying and reading my books I wouldn't be where I am now. I appreciate all of your help and support in getting me and my books out there.

My beta readers, thank you for being completely honest and for all of your feedback regarding this book.

Finally, I'd like to thank all of you for buying my books and helping me on my way to my dream job of becoming an author.

Now, I'll leave you all in peace to enjoy the second instalment of the South Coast Brothers.

Happy reading.

Chapter 1

Heather

Cammie, Liam and I pulled up in front of the main gates to the Cornish Crusaders MC. The car was loaded with as much stuff as we could possibly fit in. I wound down my window as the prospect stood by the side of my car with his arms folded across his large chest. He was tall and built, like a brick house, with no tattoos in sight.

"Hi, I'm here to see Daisy. She's my sister," I told him.

"Moving in?" he chuckles, eyebrows raised high up on his head. I smiled nervously at him and prayed that he let us in.

"Name?"

"Heather," I told him, just as Liam started to cry. His head snapped to the backseat of the car.

"You bringing that in?" he asked, screwing up his face.

"He's my son, so yes," I snapped. "If Daisy isn't around, call Mason… Um, Holes, please."

"You know the VP?" he asked, leaning his arm on the roof of the car above my door.

"VP?" I asked. "I thought Ryan was VP?"

"Na, he was shot and killed a few weeks ago. Holes got promoted." He shrugged his shoulders and walked back towards the gate where there was a small shed. He talked into what looked like a walkie talkie. I was surprised to hear about Ryan, why hadn't Daisy told me about that when I saw her at the party. Why was she at a party if she was grieving for her husband? Blade hadn't died, he left me and my world felt like it was falling apart. I didn't know how I was going to cope without him.

"Ok, go on in," he said as he slammed his hand down on the roof of the car, making me jump and Liam cry louder. I glared at him and he raised his hands in front of him as an apology. I drove up the steep driveway that led to the clubhouse and was surprised to see Mason standing there waiting for us. As soon as I turned the ignition off, he had my door open and was pulling me out of the car. He held me tight against him. "I knew you'd come back," he whispered into my hair. I pulled away from him as Liam let out a small scream. I opened the back door and pulled him out of his car seat and held him close to my chest, rubbing his back. "Where's your husband?" I didn't feel like talking about it, I knew as soon as I did that I would be a mess again.

"Where's Daisy? What happened to Ryan?" I asked, avoiding his question.

"She's in there," he pointed over his shoulder. I went to walk by and he grabbed hold of my arm. "I wouldn't, she's busy."

"What?" I asked, not sure if what I was hearing was right.

"She's got a new man already?"

"Not one, several," he laughed.

"You've got her being a club whore?" I snapped, looking up at him as he was taller than me. My head only came to his chest.

"It was her choice, sweetheart." He shrugged his shoulders.

"Heather?" Cammie said. I spun around and she was standing by the boot of the car.

"Well, well. Who's this?" Mason asked as he strolled towards Cammie. She shrunk back against the car as if she was scared. I pulled at the back of his leather cut until he stopped walking and looked around at me. I shook my head slightly, telling him not to bother her.

"What's your name, babe?" he asked her, completely ignoring me.

"C-Cammie," she stuttered. He reached out to touch her and she yelped and jumped back, fear was in her eyes when she realised she couldn't get any further away.

"I'm not gonna hurt you," he said softly.

"Mason!" I shouted out. He looked at me. "Can we stay? For a little while?"

"Absolutely." He smiled, leaving Cammie and coming back to me. I heard the roar of bikes and looked over my shoulder to see three bikes riding into the compound. Cammie quickly rushed over to me and I passed her Liam. I knew he would keep her calm and pre-occupied.

"What's going on, brother?" One of them asked. He was tall, muscly, but not broad, and had tattoos visible on his neck and hands.

"Toes, Solar, Tat. This is Heather and Cammie. They're going to be staying with us for a little while." He introduced us and I smiled at them.

"Great, fresh meat." Solar grinned.

"No..." I began to say when Mason put his hand up to stop me.

"They are not fresh meat, they are not club whores. They are off limits." Mason warned them.

"You spoil all our fun." Toes complained.

"Really? So you won't want to attend the party this evening then?" he asked them.

"Fresh meat?" Solar asked. Mason nodded and they high fived as they walked past us and into the clubhouse.

"What a bunch of jerks," I mumbled to myself.

"Hey, they're good guys. Better than that Devon lot you were hanging out with. Speaking of which, why are you here?"

"Uh, Heather. He needs changing." Cammie told me, I smiled at her in appreciation; she knew I wouldn't want to talk about it yet.

"Where are we sleeping?" I asked Mason.

"Open the boot, I'll grab some of your shit and show you."

Once we all had something in our hands to carry, we entered the clubhouse and I was thankful to see that the bar area was empty. It looked a lot nicer than the Devon MC, this place had a long bar at one side, tables scattered around the room, two large sofas that faced a large flat screen TV and a corner that looked like it was full of children's toys and books.

"Are there other kids that live here?" I asked as we followed Mason down a long corridor, doors on both sides of the walls. "Yeah, Prez and his Old Lady have three kids, Olivia, she is four. Danny, he is two and Caitlyn, she's ten months, I think." He shrugged his shoulders and pushed open a door. "This is the only one that is left, hope you don't mind sharing?"

Cammie and I both shook our heads, we would prefer to be close together. The room was quite big, it had two single beds, a wardrobe, chest of drawers and an en-suite bathroom.

"I'll leave you to settle in, we eat at six. We all eat together. I'll let everyone know that you are here."

"Thank you," I said as I reached up, gave Mason a hug and a kiss on the cheek.

"No worries. Bye." He smiled at Cammie and she smiled back at him, shyly.

Chapter 2

Mason

I walked out of their bedroom, let out a deep exhale as I leant my back against the wall by the side of their door. I let my head drop back and I smiled to myself. I was really happy to see Heather pull up, I always thought we had some unfinished business, especially after the way we broke up years ago. But as soon as I laid my eyes on Cammie, I was like, Heather who? She was gorgeous with long blonde hair, blue eyes and she was petite. There was something behind those gorgeous blue eyes of hers, she seemed troubled, afraid and untrusting. I don't recall ever seeing this girl before, how did Heather know her? And why would she be here with her?

"VP?" I heard someone call out, I looked to my left and saw the Prez nod his head, telling me he wanted to talk.

"What's up, Prez?" I asked as we walked into his office. Carla, his Old Lady was in there breast feeding Caitlyn. She wasn't bothered if any of us were around, if her baby girl needed food, she got it.

"I hear we have some visitors?" He waved his hand in the air, waiting for me to explain.

"Yeah, Daisy's sister and friend. They have nowhere else to go, I told them they could stay." I shrugged my shoulders.

"Isn't that something that I should decide on as this is my club?" he shouted, standing to his feet.

"Mike, calm down, you'll give yourself a heart attack." Carla said to him. The Prez was in his early fifties, Carla was thirty three. They had met one night when the club brothers were out on the piss and she captured his heart from the start.

"Ok, fine. But if I find them causing trouble…"

"You won't." I cut him off, standing up.

"They will have to help out around here, cleaning, cooking, shit like that. We don't need any more club whores causing us trouble." I nodded my head and he dismissed me. I walked into the bar area and Missy and Penny were cleaning down the bar and re-stocking it.

"Getting ready for tonight, girls?" I asked as I sat on one of the bar stools. They both smiled and nodded at me, Missy and Penny were our newest club bunnies. They had only been around for a few weeks so they were new to the party experience.

"Drink?" Missy purred. I nodded my head, she turned around and bent to the bottom fridge, digging out my favourite beer. I openly admired her ass, I was the first one to introduce her to club life, shortly followed by Penny and then we all had a little fun together. That was one night I'd never forget.

***

Heather

"You ok?" I asked Cammie as I sat on my bed facing her, she was laying on hers with her eyes closed.

"Yes," she whispered.

Bang. Bang. Bang.

"Open up." I heard Daisy call out. Cammie yelped and sat up in bed, looking worried.

"It's just Daisy," I told Cammie as I placed my hand on shoulder in a soothing gesture. I walked to the door and swung it open.

"Ohmygod, what are you doing here?" She squealed as she threw her arms around me. I held on tight to her as the tears began to flow down my cheeks. I sobbed and Daisy pulled away, looking at me. "What's happened?" I shook my head as I cried in front of her. "Oh, come here." She dragged me to my bed and we sat down, her arms still tight around me.

"Blade left." I heard Cammie tell her. "She woke up in the clubhouse, he had packed his stuff, told the Prez he was back to being an enforcer and left without saying anything."

"Oh, honey." Daisy comforted me.

"I thought he loved me," I cried. "And Liam."

"Liam?" Daisy asked, pulling back from me. I nodded my head towards his moses basket and Daisy got to her feet. She walked over to him and the love she had for her nephew was all over her face. I felt bad that she would never get to experience that, having a baby growing inside of you. "He's gorgeous, looks just like you."

"What happened to Ryan?" I asked.

"Not really sure, they said he got shot when they were out on a mission. Club business and all that." She waved her hand in the air like it didn't mean anything.

"When?"

"A few weeks ago. I'm ok…" She paused. "You looking forward to the party tonight? It's gonna be wild." She smiled, brightly. Any trace of sadness erased from her face. I nodded, I didn't want to tell her that we would probably be hiding, staying out of the way. The last thing we needed was to be mistaken for a club whore.

Chapter 3

Mason

The party was in full swing, we always opened our bar up to the locals in Portwrinkle so they had a place to drink and relax. Some of the locals weren't brave enough as they thought we were a typical biker club. We weren't. Yeah, we did get into some sticky situations, but we didn't use women, disrespect them or keep them against their will. The club bunnies chose to be here and in exchange for pleasing some of the men, bikers or locals they had a place to stay and food to eat. We only had four bunnies, Missy, Penny, Shelley and Lottie. They were all longing for the life of an Old Lady, but our guys weren't interested in settling down. Then there was Daisy, who was an Old Lady but her husband got killed. Carla, the Prez's Old Lady, and Amy, who's Bangers Old Lady; he is the oldest member of the club and an original Cornish Crusader.

"Hey, Holes." Missy winked at me as she passed me a beer. I nodded my head in thanks, keeping my eyes on the hallway entrance, I was waiting for a certain blonde. I was excited when Drake, the new prospect, called and said that Heather was here, I told him to let her straight in and I had convinced myself she had come back to me. That we were going to be together again after all these years, there was still something between us, I could feel it. Now I believe that something is a strong friendship, as soon as my eyes landed on Cammie, sensations flowed through my body so strong that I thought I was going to pass out. Was it love at first sight? Did I believe in that? I shook my head and chuckled to myself, I had seen this girl once over four hours ago and she had me all tied up in knots. I took my eyes away from the door and snapped them back quickly as if I was going to miss something. I was missing something, the kick ass party that was flowing all around me. There were girls, booze, music and poker, what more could a man want. 'That little blonde' the voice in my head said. I chuckled to myself once again, grabbed Penny on my way to the dance floor and started to enjoy my night.

***

Heather

"Do you want to go and join the party?" Cammie asked me. I looked towards the door where I could hear the music pumping, I was glad that Mason had put us in a room at the back of the clubhouse so Liam wasn't disturbed. He was fast asleep in his moses basket. "I don't mind staying and looking after him, I'm probably gonna have an early night anyway." She shrugged her shoulders.
"No, I'm good. Don't feel much like partying." I laid back on my bed and looked at the ceiling. Where was he? Why had he left? Would I be able to move on? Was he coming back? My thoughts got interrupted when there was a small knock on the door. From the corner of my eye I saw Cammie's posture stiffen, I needed to think of a way to calm her, to make her relax. I got up from the bed and opened the door, Daisy came bounding in.
"Sshh, Liam's asleep," I told her quietly before she made too much noise.
"What are you doing in here? Come and have a drink," she slurred.
"How much have you had to drink?" I asked, watching her sway on the spot.

"Only a couple, it helps you know. To not remember him." I assumed she was talking about her husband. Maybe she had a point, maybe I would be able to sleep better tonight if I was drunk.

"We could lock the room and take the baby monitor with us," I said to Cammie. She shook her head and I knew it was no use trying to convince her. "Shit, I don't have anything to wear."

"Let's go via my room and get you one of my dresses." I nodded at her and turned back towards Cammie to make sure it was ok.

"Don't say anything, just go. I'm gonna lock the door behind you so you'll have to knock when you come back." I gave her a small smile, skipped towards her and gave her a big hug. "I just want to forget him, at least for a little while," I whispered to her. She nodded her head as she knew that's what I needed. I walked over to Liam, bent down, kissed his little head and told him I loved him. "If you need me, come and get me." Cammie gave me a smile, and as Daisy and I left the room I heard the lock being turned. The music was a lot louder the closer we got to the bar. We stopped at a door and Daisy pushed it open. It was bare, it looked like no one lived in it. There was a double bed, a chest of drawers under the window and a small wardrobe along the same wall as the bathroom door.

"Was this your room with Ryan?" I asked as she dug around in her wardrobe looking for something for me to wear.

"No, the VP has a large room. Holes has that room now."

"He chucked you out? Where are all of your things?" I asked as I looked around.

"Burnt it all. It just kept reminding me of him... Oh, here, this one is perfect for you." She handed me a black, short strapless dress. I took it from her and changed quickly.

"Is it too short?" I asked, trying to look behind me to see if my ass was falling out.

"No, put these heels on." She pushed some red, four inch heels towards me and for once I looked and felt sexy. I couldn't wear a bra as I didn't have a strapless one, luckily the dress had built in support. "You look hot! Fluff that hair up and I'll grab you some mascara and lipstick."

Once I was ready, we headed out of Daisy's room and into the bar, it was packed. A lot more people than the Devon MC ever had. We walked over to the long bar and there were three girls serving so it didn't take long for us to get a drink. Daisy ordered a bottle of wine and two glasses.

"I don't have any money," I told her.

"It goes on the club tab. Only the locals pay for their drinks, and at dirt cheap prices too." I looked around and there was some guys playing poker in the corner of the room. A lot of people were dancing on the dance floor as the DJ had some good tunes on. I could see a couple sitting together in a booth, they looked very much in love and it had me wondering who they were.

"Who's that?" I asked as I followed Daisy to a table so we could start drinking the wine she ordered.

"That's the Prez and his Old Lady, Carla... You know he is twenty years older than her."

"Really?" I asked, looking at her. That surprised me, you could see there was an age difference but I didn't think it would be that much.

"Hey, ladies." I heard. I looked up and saw Mason had pulled a chair up and joined us, he was laid back and casual sitting in his chair. He smiled at me, I smiled back but I didn't want to give him the wrong impression. I know Blade had left me, but that didn't stop me still wanting him to walk in that door and claim me all over again. It didn't stop my heart beating for only him. I didn't want to be thinking about this. I grabbed my full glass of wine and downed the lot, holding it out for Daisy to fill it up.

"Hey, sweetheart, slow down there. When was the last time

you had a drink?" I shrugged my shoulders. It was definitely a while ago, way before I got pregnant with Liam. "Maybe you should slow down," he said taking the glass away from me.

"Leave her alone, if she wants to drink, let her." Daisy snapped at him. She knew my pain, she knew how I felt. Though knowing your husband was dead has got to be ten times worse, even more than that. I couldn't bear the thought that something like that had happened to Blade.

"Hey, sexy, want to dance?" I looked up and the guy that I had met earlier was standing in front of me. What was his name?

"Solar." Mason said in a warning tone. That's it, Solar. I looked at him, nodded and placed my hand in his.

"I'm only dancing with her, man." He led me to the middle of the dance floor and we danced close together, not really touching.

"Solar? That's a different name," I said as we danced.

"Yeah, I got named that when the guys realised that I always liked to fuck in the mornings." He smirked at me and winked.

"Oh, really?" I purred as I stepped in closer to him. "Mornings don't really work for me." I wound my arms around his neck. He pulled back, spun me around and pulled me flush against his body. I could feel his hardness through his jeans and rubbed my ass over him, I wanted to forget Blade and what better way than this.

Mason

Heather was at the party so that meant that Cammie must have been looking after the baby. I needed to see her so I headed to their bedroom. Once I was stood outside, I felt nervous, what was I going to say to her? Get a grip, you're the VP of an MC. It's only a chick. I raised my hand and knocked gently on the door. I heard some movements and some muttering, but with the background noise from the party I couldn't hear anything.

"That was quick, Heath..." Cammie started saying and she stopped talking when she saw that it was me. Her posture stiffened and she started backing away from me. I wasn't sure if that was an invite in, I stepped over the threshold and looked around. The baby was asleep and I closed the door behind me so he wouldn't be disturbed by the noise.

"W...what do you want?" Cammie asked, her voice sounded unsure.

"I needed to see you." I stalked towards her and she fell onto her bed, backing herself up against the headboard.

"Please, don't," she cried, "not with Liam in here." She held her hands out in front of her, trying to keep me away. I took a step back and really looked at her. She was pale, shaking and tears were running down her face.

"Babe, I'm not going to hurt you," I told her gently as I sat opposite her on the other bed, resting my forearms on my knees with my head dipped.

"What do you want then?" she asked again, pulling her knees up and wrapping her arms around them.

"I just wanted to come and see you. Why aren't you at the party?" She looked over towards Liam. "He's Heather's kid, why are you stuck looking after him?"

"I'm not stuck looking after him," she snapped. I cocked my head to the side, eyebrows raised and looked at her. "Sorry," she whispered, resting her head on her knees. I moved closer towards her and sat on her bed beside her hip. I wanted to push her chin up so I could see those mesmerising blue eyes, but thought I shouldn't. She was clearly scared and I wanted to know why.

"Why are you scared?" I asked.

"I'm not scared!" she bit out as she jumped up from the bed and put some distance between us.

"I could see it, when you were eating with us earlier. You kept your head down, didn't hardly touch your food and jumped when someone came too close to you." She walked towards Liam and looked down at him, smiling. What I would give to have her smile at me like that.

"What happened to you?" I asked, standing up and facing her. I wanted to pull her close to me and kiss those pink lips, I wanted to feel her curves under my hands and hear her moan my name.

"Holes, I think you should leave," she said.

"Mason," I told her. She looked at me confused. "It's my name, call me Mason."

"Ok," she whispered, looking down at Liam again. She had longing in her eyes and I wondered if that's what she was looking for a family of her own. She didn't look very old, no more than twenty I would have thought.

"Talk to me, tell me about you. What happened to you?"

"Get out," she sneered.

"Babe," I said in a warning tone, no one spoke to the Prez, VP or a club brother like that.

"I said get out. GET OUT! GET OUT! GET OUT!" she screamed at me, causing the baby to wake up screaming. She picked him up and held him close to her chest. She turned her back on me and I backed away to the door and left. She had got under my skin, I wanted to be near her, to touch her, to taste her. My cock was rock hard. I stood outside of her door, shaking my head when I felt a hand snake around my waist. I looked over my shoulder and was pleased to see that it was Penny. She was the only one out of the club bunnies that was blonde.

"Fuck me," she whispered. I smirked at her and winked, she took hold of my hand and began heading towards my bedroom. I didn't want to take her in there, I wanted to save that room and my bed for only Cammie. I steered her in the direction of the gym, it would be empty this time of night.

Once we walked in the door, I pulled her back up against my chest and growled in her ear;

"Are you ready for me?"

"Hmm mmm, I'm soaking wet for you, Holes," she purred. I walked forward, moving her at the same time and pushed her down onto the training mats. She fell onto her hands and knees.

"Stay there, in that position," I demanded. She knew better than to disobey me. All I could see was a sexy body and a head full of blonde hair. I palmed my cock through my jeans, I needed a release and quick, it was starting to become painful. I pulled my jeans and boxers down my legs and knelt down behind her. I quickly slid a condom on and pushed her skirt up to her waist, I was impressed to see that she wasn't wearing any underwear and she was bare for me. Her swollen pussy and clit were calling out to me. I didn't hesitate, I grabbed her hips and slammed into her, causing her to scream out.

"You ok?" I asked.

"Mmm," she moaned and nodded her head. I had been with Penny several times before, she was used to my size and piercings. I just hoped that Cammie would be able to take me just as well. When the time was right. "Holes," she moaned, moving herself against me.

"Quiet!" I snapped, thrusting into her. She dipped her head onto the mat below us and I grabbed her pretty blonde hair, wrapped it around my fist and pulled her head up. Slamming into her hard and fast. I didn't want to hear her voice, I wanted to imagine I was fucking Cammie, fucking her tight warm hole as I pulled at her gorgeous blonde hair. Taking her pleasure to the maximum and forcing orgasm after orgasm out of her body.

"Yes, yes, yes. Holes, fuck me, fuck me, fuck me," she called out, over and over again. She was making it difficult to think of Cammie. I forced myself into her harder and harder until I heard her scream out in pleasure, I pulled out of her, my cock still hard, pulled up my jeans and walked away. My cock only wanted one blonde now and I couldn't get her out of my head.

Chapter 4

Heather

"Where are we going?" I asked as I climbed into the back of my car with Liam. Mason said he was taking us out, along with Cammie and demanded to drive. I was getting used to all these guys having their own way.

"I'll sit in the back with him," Cammie said as I pulled my seat belt on and was about to close the door.

"It's ok, I'm here now. You sit in the front with Mason." I smiled and she quickly glanced at Mason and then back to me, she nodded her head and climbed into the car. I had noticed something brewing between them, a lot of side glances and Mason was always near her. I even heard Penny, one of the bunnies complaining to the other girls that a couple of nights ago Mason fucked her in the gym, made her come and then left without saying a word. Apparently he was known for sticking around for round two.

"I'm taking you out to lunch, to properly welcome you girls here and the newest member of our club," he chuckled, pointing towards Liam.

"No way is my son *ever* going to be in a MC," I told him, shaking my head. Mason chuckled again as we set off into town.

"What's wrong with being in a MC?" Mason asked. "You didn't mind when it was your last two men."

"Mason!" Cammie hissed at him.

"It's ok, I'll tell you why. The first one lied to me about being in the club and the second one left without saying goodbye.

That shows you the kind of men that are in these clubs."

"Hey!" Mason objected. "I'm not like them."

"Oh, really? So I didn't see you at the sex party at the Devon Destroyers then?"

"I was having a bit of fun. If I had the right girl, someone I wanted to be my Old Lady then I would treat her right, protect her and never stray." I saw him look out of the corner of his eye towards Cammie. She was looking down at her hands, twisting them in her lap. I really needed to talk to her about what was going on with them.

Ring. Ring. Ring. Ring.

"Shit." Mason swore as his phone started ringing. He pulled over to the side of the road and dug his phone out of his pocket. "Yeah?" he answered. "Now? I'll be right there." He sighed deeply. Once he hung up the phone, he dropped it into the cup holder and carried on driving. "We have to make a de tour."

"Where to?" I asked, leaning forward in my seat so I could hear him better.

"Never you mind," he growled. I looked at Cammie and she was looking at him too, I could see her lip twitching like she wanted to say something. She never would have answered back to the club brothers as she knew her place, but I got the feeling she wanted to argue with Mason just to rile him up. I smiled at the thought, it meant I was getting my Cammie back.

We turned down a dirt road and pulled up in front of a large building, it was painted white and a line of bikes were lined up outside of it.

"I won't be long. Stay here," he said looking between me and Cammie. We both nodded and he climbed out of the car and walked away. Cammie turned in her seat and looked over at Liam, smiling when she saw that he was fast asleep.

"What's going on with you two?" I asked, not beating around the bush. She looked down and she was worrying her lip between her teeth. "Talk to me, do you like him?"

"I… I think so. I'm not sure, he's sweet." She looked at me. "He scared the hell out of me a couple days ago when he came to our room when you were at the party. I thought he was going to hurt me, take what he wanted from me."

"He's not like that," I told her, placing my hand over hers. Mason was a good guy, he cared about people, and he wouldn't hurt her intentionally. But then, what did I know, Blade said he would never hurt me and that's exactly what he did. They're meant to protect their Old Ladies and he just up and left me and Liam.

"But to him, I'm probably just a club whore, someone to have a good time with and I can't even give him that… Not yet."

"Talk to him, tell him how you feel. Does he know what happened?" She shook her head wildly.

"He doesn't need to know." She turned herself around in her seat, ending the conversation. I pressed my back into the car seat and looked over at Liam. He was sleeping peacefully, not a care in the world. I had to stay strong, for him. He needed me and I couldn't break down and stop caring for him. It still hurt like hell, Blade leaving us, my heart was in pieces and I didn't know how I was going to get over him. Time was a healer, that's what people said. It had only been a week.

***

We had been sitting in the car waiting for Mason for over an hour.

"I'm going to find him," I said as I pushed my door open and stepped out. Liam had woken up ten minutes ago and Cammie was trying to entertain him, he was getting fussy and I didn't want to be sitting around waiting for Mason. If he was busy then I'd take the car and come and pick him up later. I walked towards the main door and pushed it open. I came to a small reception area with a few scattered chairs and no one sitting at the desk. I furrowed my brow and carried on walking. The next room I came to was an office, with a large mahogany desk, a small sofa and several book cases, the room was empty so I carried on through the next door. I walked into what looked like a cinema room, there was rows of chairs and a large flat screen TV on the wall. I thought it was strange at how all of these rooms were empty. I carried on and as I was about to open up the next door I could hear voices, one sounding like Mason. I pushed the door open and came into a large open space, I looked around and there were several little rooms covering all the walls, with no doors. All I saw was women, scantily dressed and talking to themselves.

"Ah, she's perfect," a man called out as he walked towards me, "Dom must have sent her." He grabbed the top of my arm and began dragging me towards another room. Just as we were about to walk in, Mason looked over his shoulder and his eyes connected with mine.

"Nope, she's here for me," he said as he stepped closer to the older man, who had a fake tan and overly bright clothes on.

"You can't have her, just because you want her for yourself. We need another girl for the scene."

"The scene? What's going on? What is this place?" I asked, looking around. Mason stepped closer to me and pulled me away from the other guy.

"She's an Old Lady. She's looking for me," he growled and the other guy stepped away, hands raised in surrender. Mason spun me around to look at me. "What are you doing in here?"

"I came to look for you, Liam is fussing and I need to feed him. What is this place?" I asked, looking around again.

"It's club business," he answered.

"Don't give me none of that shit, tell me." He sighed and rubbed his hand on the back of his neck. He stepped closer to me so only I could hear him.

"You need to remember, I am the VP of the club that took you in, giving you a place to stay, food to eat. You *do not* talk to me like that, got it?" He surprised me, he had never spoken to me that way before, maybe I was wrong about him, maybe Cammie shouldn't trust him. I lowered my head, not looking at him, turned around and started walking away.

"Heather," he called out on a sigh. I stopped in my tracks, I had to obey him; we had no-where else to go. I'd do what was needed to keep a roof over my head for my son. I felt him at my back and his hands ran up and down my arms soothingly, trying to calm me down. "I'm sorry," he apologised.

"Doesn't matter," I muttered, not turning around. I wouldn't get too attached to any of these guys, I didn't know when any of them would up and leave, get killed or throw us out. I'd do what I was told until I could figure out a plan. I stepped away from him and he grabbed a hold of my hand.

"I'll tell you." He spun me around to look at him.

"No, I know my place. I'm no longer an Old Lady." I turned back around and pulled my hand free from him.

"Well, look who's here." Solar smirked as he walked towards us. "Getting in the porn business?" he asked, cocking his head to the side.

"That's what this is?" I asked, eyes wide from my surprise.

"Yep. Let me show you around." He winked at me, took hold of my hand and led me to each room. "This is Kitty, she's in the cleaning room." I looked at him confused. "There's a web cam set up, guys log on to the website and pay to watch her clean in a skimpy outfit." He wiggled his eyebrows at me.

"That's it, that's all she does? She gets paid for that?" He nodded and led me to another room. This one had a woman dressed in leather and holding a whip.

"This is Dana in our dominatrix room, she pretends to whip the guys, giving them orders. It's one of the rooms with microphones," he whispered. I nodded, understanding that he didn't want me to speak. We walked away and I asked;

"So, they just get watched? No actual physical contact?"

"It depends on how much they are looking to make. This

room," he nodded his head to the right and we walked in that direction, "Is one of the highest paid jobs." I looked into the room and saw a man stretched out on what looked like a massage table, he had one girl sitting on his face and the other straddled his hips. They were both moving and moaning. I looked at Solar and he put his finger over his lips telling me to be quiet. I went to walk away when he stopped me, he stood behind me and I felt his lips brush against my ear.

"These girls get to have fun and make money. It's hot, isn't it?" I squirmed in front of him. My body burned and tingled with excitement. He led me away and once we were nowhere near that room, I stopped him.

"What was up the other night?" I asked. He looked at me blankly. "I threw myself at you and you walked away. You show me around here, get me hot and bothered by standing so close and..."

"I'm not looking for an Old Lady," he snapped.

"I don't want to be one, I just want to have some fun!" I shouted back, remembering that I wasn't supposed to talk to the brothers this way.

"Well, you won't be getting much fun at the clubhouse." He walked away and I ran to catch up with him, pulled on his arm to stop him from walking.

"What does that mean?" He looked over his shoulder and then back at me.

"We've had our orders to stay away from you and Cammie."

"WHAT?" I screamed, looking around for Mason. I couldn't see him anywhere so I stormed back to the car. He was outside talking to Cammie who had Liam cradled in her arms. I was fuming and I didn't care how I wasn't supposed to talk to him. "MASON!" He looked up as I ran towards him. "How dare you warn the guys off us, if I want to have some fun it should be my choice, no one else's." Cammie looked up at Mason when I shouted at him.

"You warned them off both of us?" she asked.

"Yeah, you're mine," he said looking at Cammie, "and I didn't want you making a mistake, one you would regret with a one night stand," he said to me. I looked at Cammie and I couldn't tell if she was pissed at what he said or if she was happy about it.

"That's my decision to make!" I snapped.

"Heather, he's coming back." Cammie said as she grabbed hold of one of my hands.

"What?" I whispered. Had she spoken to him? Did she know he was leaving?

"He'll be back, I just know he will be. He wouldn't leave you and Liam." I shook my head.

"He's gone. Forever." I grabbed Liam and got back in the car. I didn't feel like going out for the day, I wanted to go and hide away from everyone for a few hours.

Chapter 5

Mason

The girls had been living at the clubhouse for a month, they had settled in well. They helped out with the cooking and cleaning in exchange for a place to stay and money. I was waiting in the tattoo/piercing shop that we had on the compound, I was waiting for a customer when I heard the bell on the door chime. I looked up and into a set of bright blue eyes, my face erupted into a large smile. I stood up and made my way towards Cammie. I leant down to give her a gentle kiss on the lips and pulled her in close for a cuddle. I always felt better when I had her in my arms. She came to me a couple of weeks ago and laid it all out there, told me that she was feeling things for me she had never felt before and that it scared her. She said she had been through a rough time and she wasn't ready for a physical relationship. I had hoped she would have told me what had happened but she didn't. I wouldn't push her, she'd tell me when the time was right. She made it clear that she would not tolerate me sleeping with other people, especially the club bunnies. I hadn't had sex for over five weeks, after that experience with Penny I didn't bother again. I only wanted Cammie and for now my only release was my own hand.

"What you doing here?" I asked her.

"I've come to clean up," she smiled at me.

"Babe, this place is cleaner than the kitchen," I chuckled. "It has to be sterile."

"Oh, I'll leave you to it then." She went to walk away as the door opened and she came face to face with a dark haired girl, tanned complexion and not a lot of clothing.

"Hi, I'm here for my eleven o'clock appointment." She had a high pitched voice that went straight through me, like nails on a chalk board.

"Nice to meet you," I said as I shook her hand. She stepped in closer to me, not releasing my hand and whispered in my ear.

"The pleasure is all mine. I want to suck your cock as a way of appreciation." I cleared my throat, pulled my hand out of hers and stepped away.

"Go on in and make yourself comfortable." I pointed to the room where I had my equipment set up.

"What is she having done?" Cammie asked, hands on her hips.

"She's having her clit pierced," I told her.

"Oh." She bit the inside of her lip and looked down at the floor.

"You're not jealous, are you?" I smirked as I pulled her lip free and kissed her.

"Of having a needle shoved through my clit, I don't think so," she scoffed.

"It won't take long. Wait here for me?" I asked her. She nodded and made herself comfortable behind the counter. Flicking through an old magazine, a motorcycle one. I laughed and walked back into the room to get this over with.

Heather

I decided I wanted to do something different and daring today. I had a rough couple of days, missing Blade and not knowing what I was going to do with my life, my future. I headed into the tattoo/ piercing shop, which funnily enough didn't have a name. People called it the CC shop.

"Hey, what are you doing here?" I asked as I walked in the door and saw Cammie sitting behind the counter.

"Mase is working, he asked me to stay. What are you doing here? Where's Liam?"

"He's asleep so Carla said she would watch him."

"So, what are you doing here?" she asked again.

"I…"

"I said no! GET THE FUCK OUT!" We both looked towards the back room when we heard Mason's booming voice shouting. A few seconds later a girl walked out, looking uncomfortable, threw some money at Cammie and stormed away. We both waited for Mason to appear and when he didn't we walked back to his room.

"You ok?" Cammie asked, walking towards him. He pulled her in close to him and placed his lips on her neck. I had seen him do this a couple of times, it was almost like a way for him to calm down. She cradled his head close to her, running her hands through his dark hair.

"What happened?" I asked, breaking the silence.

"Stupid bitch wanted to suck my cock."

"Oh, how terrible for you," I laughed. Which caused Cammie to giggle too. They broke apart and he did not look impressed.

"There is only one set of lips I want wrapped around my cock," he said as he swept his finger over Cammie's bottom lip.

"Sorry, been there, done that," I giggled. He shot a warning glare at me and I silenced my giggling. When Cammie finally admitted her feelings for Mason she came to me, to ask if it would make things weird between us as I had dated him previously. I told her not to worry about it at all, that I saw him more like a best friend now and we were together over ten years ago. He would always be special to me, we both lost our virginity to each other, but that seemed like a whole other life ago.

"What you doing here?" Mason asked, looking at me.

"I want a piercing," I told him. His eyebrows rose and he cocked his head to the side. "I want my tongue and nipples pierced."

"You can't breastfeed if you have them pierced," he told me.

"I don't breastfeed."

"Are you sure about this?" Cammie asked, stepping closer to me and away from Mason. I nodded my head.

"Well, sit in the chair then." Mason said as he patted the seat for me. "Which do you want doing first?"

"Which one hurts more?" I asked. He shrugged his shoulder. "Come on, you've had both done."

"You have your nipples pierced?" Cammie asked him.

"Just one. I didn't have the barbell in the other night," he winked at her and she blushed.

"Do my tongue first," I said. I sat back in the chair and thought it couldn't have hurt any more than childbirth, right? Half an hour later and I was all done. "Your tongue swelling will go down in about ten days. Make sure you keep your nipples well cleaned, use this solution on them in the shower. Don't play with the barbells as you can infect them and a salt water solution will help speed up the healing time."

"What is the healing time?"

"For your tongue, about three weeks. For your nipples, between six to eight weeks." I nodded and we all left the shop. Mason and Cammie hand in hand.

Chapter 6

Mason

We were sitting in a church meeting when the intercom buzzed and I was closest to it so I stood up and pressed the button. I was happy this morning, lying in bed with my girl, I had put a claim on her last week, officially. After she had shown me her jealousy side in my shop, I knew she was the one for me. I didn't want to scare her off with the Old Lady title quite yet.

"This better be good, we're in the middle of church," I growled to Drake, the prospect that was manning the gates.

"Sorry, VP. The police are here."

"Have you let them in?" I asked.

"No, I wanted to contact you first."

"They're the police, you always let them in. We ain't got nothing to hide." I shook my head at the no common sense coming from this guy. I turned back towards the table. "Pigs are here."

Prez slammed his gavel down on the table and we all exited the room closing the door behind us. If you weren't a member of the club, you wouldn't know there was a door there, it blended in with the walls. The room was for club brothers only. We weren't phased by the police turning up, we had a guy on the inside, Brett. He's a biker, joins in with parties when he isn't on shift. We had nothing to hide, the porn business was all legit and we had partnerships in strip clubs and dance clubs, which kept us ticking over nicely. Our hands weren't tied in nothing illegal at present. I headed towards the main doors, Prez and the brothers following. I was pleased to see Brett climbing out of his car along with a female police officer. She was tall, slim with short dark hair. I saw out of the corner of my eye Tat and Toes rubbing their hands together, they started jeering and cat calling. The Prez soon shut them up and ordered them inside.

"Brett, good to see you, man," I said as we shook hands.

"Alright?" he asked in his Cornish accent. Shaking Prez's hand too. The female officer stayed near the car.

"Yeah, we're good. What can we do for you?" Prez asked him.

"Is there somewhere we can talk?" he asked, leaning in closer. Prez nodded his head towards the clubhouse and we followed him in.

"Girls, OUT!" Prez shouted into the bar. I saw Cammie look up at me, I nodded my head and she and Heather left the room along with the other Old Ladies and club bunnies. We walked further into the room. "Have a seat." Prez said. "Want a drink?"

"No, I'm fine." He sat down, Prez sitting opposite him, me and the rest of the brothers stood around waiting to hear what he was going to say.

"Get on." Prez said, I chuckled at his way of telling Brett to hurry up and tell us what is going on.

"I need your help… We've heard about a sex trafficking place, but can we find it? Nope, it's like a needle in a haystack. Have you guys heard anything? If I can find this place, it'll be great for my career."

"Not heard a thing. Toes get on that computer of yours and see if you can find anything out." Prez ordered.

"On it," he replied.

"Any idea who's involved?" I asked. He shook his head.

"You've not given us much info." Prez complained. "When you have more, contact us and we'll see what we can do." Brett nodded as he stood up.

"You got my number if Toes comes up with anything." Prez nodded and shook his hand.

"Daddy, Daddy!" Prez's son came running into the room calling for him, followed by Carla. Prez scooped him up and placed him on his shoulder.

"I'm sorry, honey. He got away from me while I was changing Caitlyn." Carla explained.

"Don't worry, sweetheart. I was just coming to find you. Think we can get the girls to look after them for an hour?" He winked at her.

"I'll sort it," she said as she pulled Danny off Prez's shoulders and walked away.

"Get the info." Prez shouted at Toes before he walked away after his wife.

"Will we see you at the party next week?" I asked Brett as I walked him out, a few of the brothers were outside smoking.

"Yeah, see you dreckly," he said as he got in the car.

"What the hell is dreckly?" Solar asked, looking confused.

"Dreckly means I'll do it soon or I'll see you soon. No actual time frame." I slapped Solar on the back and went in search of Cammie and Heather.

Chapter 7

Heather

Mason had managed to convince Cammie to go out to a club
with them, but she said she wouldn't go unless I was going
too. She begged and pleaded me, she was excited to go out on
Mason's arm as his woman, away from the clubhouse. Carla
had offered to look after Liam as she and Prez were going to
have a quiet night in. Even Daisy and the club bunnies were
coming with us along with the club brothers. Drake got the
raw end of the deal, as a prospect, he was made to drive us.

"Where we heading?" I asked as I climbed onto the mini bus
that was rented for us.

"Plymouth." Drake answered, starting up the bus.

"How long will that take?" Cammie asked.

"About forty minutes, babe." Mason said as he tucked her
under his arm.

"Let's go then." I called out as I slapped Drake on the back. He
started driving and it was all quiet in the bus except for the
radio. The club bunnies and Daisy were in the back of the bus,
drinking and giggling.

"Here, Heather, do you want some of this?" Penny shouted
from the back of the bus. I turned in my seat and saw her
stumbling towards me holding out a bottle with an orange
concoction in it.

"What is it?" I asked, screwing my face up as she squeezed
herself onto my seat.

"Sex on the beach."

"Oh, I want some." Cammie piped up, grabbing the bottle
from Penny.

"Hey, anyone got any money for the toll bridge?" Drake shouted from the front of the bus.

"I have." I called out as I walked up the bus to pass him some money.

"Thanks, Heather."

"No problem. How long til you patch in?" I asked as I stood beside him.

"Not a clue, until they decide I can." He shrugged his shoulders.

"Heather come and have some of this stuff, it's yummy." Cammie called out. I nodded my head and walked back towards them, grabbing the bottle and emptying its contents. By the time we arrived at the club us girls were already a little tipsy.

"Where's Solar?" I asked, only now realising he wasn't on the bus.

"He's joining us in a bit." Mason told me as I stepped off the bus and headed to the back of the queue, arm in arm with Cammie. "Ladies!" He called out, we stopped and turned around to face him. "We don't have to wait, we can go straight in." He held his hand out for Cammie, she took it but didn't let me go either.

"Is this one of your clubs?" I asked.

"Yep, we know it's a safe one. The bouncers are hand-picked by us. Only the best." I looked up at the sign before we walked in. 'Maze' what a strange name for a club. I wondered where the name came from. Once I walked inside, I got my answer. There was a long dark corridor we had to walk down and then inside there were mirrors everywhere, which made you feel a bit disorientated, like you were in a maze.

"Shit, I'm gonna walk into a mirror," I complained as we walked up to the large bar spreading across the back wall on both sides of the club so there wasn't a long wait for drinks.

"They're all along the walls, you'll be fine." Mason said, passing us all a drink. In total there was ten of us. It was busy and people were already filling up the dance floor. This was my first proper night out in ages. A clubhouse party didn't count and I was determined to enjoy it.

"Oh, I love this song. Let's dance." Daisy screamed as she grabbed mine and Cammie's hands and dragged us to the middle of the dance floor. Snap! 'Rhythm Is A Dancer' was playing and we were dancing to the beat and throwing our hands in the air, laughing and having a good time. I glanced over to the bar and saw the guys watching us, Mason was keeping a close eye on Cammie. I nodded my head at him to join us. He smiled and he, Toes and Tat strolled towards us as Rednex 'Cotton Eye Joe' re-mix came on. We all started attempting to line dance, it was funny watching the guys linking arms and swinging around. I hadn't laughed so much in ages.

"I love this old music!" I called out.

"Where did you come from, where did you go, where did you come from Cotton Eye Joe!" We all sung out together. I looked around as I felt someone watching me and didn't know if Solar had made it in yet. I couldn't see anyone so I carried on dancing and Tat started swinging me around on the dancefloor.

"I need a drink!" I called out to them and made my way to the bar. Everyone else was still dancing. I leant over the bar, making sure the barman could see the generous amount of cleavage I had on display tonight. He was smiling at me within two minutes.

"What can I get you?"

"Vodka and red bull please, double." He nodded his head and I looked to my left as I felt a hand resting on my bum. I stepped away from the guy and shook my head, he stepped closer to me again and within seconds he was being dragged away by Toes. I saw the guy look at his cut and he was soon surrendering and walking away.

"You ok?" Toes asked, standing at my side. I nodded as the

bar man passed me my drink and I downed it in one. I looked back over the dancefloor and Cammie, Mason, Penny and Tat were still dancing, Daisy had disappeared and I couldn't see her anywhere. I walked over to join them, swaying my hips to the music, Sisqo 'Thong Song'. It had a good beat to bump and grind too, it was just a shame I had no one to dance with. After a few seconds, I felt hands on my hips and a strong body against me, I went to turn around and he started moving his hips. I looked over to Cammie and she nodded in encouragement and had a big smile on her face, I thought what the hell, I was just going to enjoy it. I worked my bum into his hard cock that I could feel through his jeans. When he first started dancing with me, I was curious to what he looked like, I looked at all the mirrors around us but all I could see were the other people in the club dancing. He ran his face over my neck and his stubble tickled me, I could feel myself getting excited and turned on, I was not one for a one night stand with a stranger. As the song was finishing he spun me around so fast, grabbing hold of my hips and slammed his lips down onto mine. I knew those lips anywhere and soon my mouth opened up for him and our tongues were entwined. Was I dreaming? Was I really that drunk? I couldn't get enough of him and I wound my arms around his neck and he picked me up and I wound my legs around his back, not caring that the whole club could see my underwear. I felt him moving, not sure where we were going, we broke apart so he could see where he was walking and I trailed my lips over his chin and neck. Kissing and biting him. I heard him growl as I was pushed into a wall. We didn't talk, we kissed and we touched. Soon enough, my dress was pushed up to my waist and my underwear was ripped from my body, I looked around to make sure no one could see us, we were in a secluded dark corner and the beat from the music was vibrating off the walls. He trailed a finger over my wet folds and pushed it inside of me, I bucked my hips against his hand and he inserted another finger. Thrusting inside of me as he kissed and nibbled the sensitive area of my neck, before I knew it I was crying out. I could feel and hear the sounds of a belt being loosened and then I felt the large head of his cock at my entrance. I moved my hips, letting him know I was ready and that I wanted this. He pushed inside of me with one movement and I felt myself needing to adjust to his size. He had me stretched and I could feel myself pulsing around him. He started to move, his head resting on my shoulder and I could feel every breath on my neck; he had one hand on my hip and one on my bum. My arms were wound around his neck and he slammed into me, slamming me against the wall. It felt amazing and I knew that I would be coming again very soon. His rhythm didn't stop, he pounded in and out of me, making sure that I would still feel where he had been tomorrow. My arms tightened around his neck and my legs squeezed his waist as I felt the build-up, he pulled my legs apart further as he tucked his arm under my left leg pulling me towards him as he ploughed into me harder, I screamed out, shortly followed by him. We didn't move, we stayed still until our breathing had evened out. I was feeling more sober all of a sudden and wondered what the hell I had just done. "Put me down," I demanded smacking him lightly on the arm. As he pulled out of me I felt our combined release seeping down my leg. Once my feet hit the floor, I pulled my dress into position and ran my fingers through my hair.

"Sugar, I missed you," he whispered as he placed his forehead against mine again. I wanted to be mad at him for leaving. I found all I wanted to do was hold him close to me and beg him not to leave me again. I needed answers and I wasn't going to put up with any club business shit. "How's Liam? Who has him?"

"He's good, he…"

"Shit." Blade swore as he dug his ringing phone out of his pocket. "Sugar, I…" I cut him off by grabbing his phone to see who it was.

"Ashlyn?" I screamed at him, throwing his phone towards him. I shook my head and stormed away from him.

"Heather!" I heard him call my name but I headed straight for the exit. As soon as I was outside, I heard a rumble of a bike and was so relieved to see Solar pull up. I ran towards him, jumped on the back of his bike and screamed at him to go.

Chapter 8

Heather

I spent all night awake, every time I moved I could feel where Blade had been only hours before. His touch and kisses overwhelmed me. I loved him with all that I had, I felt a need to be close to him, I trusted him and he let me down, again. Not only had he walked out on me, but now he had fucked me against a wall in a public club while he was seeing another woman. Who the hell was Ashlyn? Why was I not enough for him? I rolled over on to my side when I heard Liam gurgling, I looked at him and he had arms and legs flying about. I pulled him into my arms and laid him on the bed next to me, he was always happy first thing, active. I looked at the clock and was surprised to see that it was already eight in the morning, normally my boy would have been awake and wanting food by now. I climbed out of bed, changed his nappy and carried him to the kitchen to get his milk ready. As it was still early, I didn't bother changing out of my sleep shorts and vest top, I didn't run a brush through my hair either. I'd be very surprised if I ran into anyone. I liked this time of the morning, just me and my boy. I made his bottle and we headed into the bar area. As Liam fed I always caught up with the news on the big screen TV. I was surprised when I walked into the room to see it wasn't empty. There was silence as I entered and I looked up to see Cammie, Mason, Daisy and Blade looking at me.

"What's he doing here?" I asked, looking at Mason. He glanced towards Blade and then back at me, his mouth opened as he was about to talk when Blade stood up and headed towards me. His eyes were focused on Liam.

"Hey, little man," he cooed as he tickled his tummy.

"Don't!" I snapped, pulling Liam up to my chest to hide him from Blade.

"Sugar..." Blade started when a cry from Liam cut him off.

"I need to feed him..."

"Let me do it, please?" Blade begged, cutting me off.

I shook my head. "No, you don't get to come in here and get him all excited to just leave again."

"I'll feed him, you need to talk." Cammie said as she pulled Liam away from me and walked back over towards Mason. I watched as Cammie got Liam comfy in her arms and placed the bottle to his lips, my greedy boy suckled on that bottle like he wasn't going to get fed again. I placed my arms around me in a protective pose. I felt uncomfortable standing in front of everyone in my PJs and looking a mess. This handsome man standing in front of me, wearing the same jeans and t-shirt with his leather cut that he had on last night, made my body tremble. I wanted him to hold me, I also wanted to scream, shout and take all my frustrations out on him.

"I haven't got time for this. You should get back to your club," I told him, sounding bored.

"Come with me," he quietly said, taking a step closer to me. I was shocked by this and my face must have mirrored that as he chuckled.

"Why would I wanna go back to that horrible place and with you?" I placed my hands on my hips as I stared at him. I saw his eyes do a sweep of my body and land on my chest, his lips curled into a smirk and I quickly crossed my arms over my chest, considering that I had a bra on, to stop the piercings catching in my clothing while I slept. I was surprised that my nipples were still visible, even when I was angry at him my body betrayed me. "I'm cold," I told him. He chuckled again, shaking his head from side to side.

"You're mine. That's why you're coming with me," he placed

his hands on my cheeks which earnt a gasp coming from me, was he going to kiss me? I didn't want him to kiss me. Or did I? "Stick out your tongue," he demanded. I pulled my head away from him and took a step away. "Sugar," he said in a warning tone and I knew better than to defy him. I stuck my tongue out at him quickly. "Fuck, that's sexy," he groaned, grabbing the front of his jeans trying to make himself more comfortable. "I want to feel that wrapped around my cock." My body tightened at the thought, a pulsing shot straight to my core and I felt myself tremble. "You're mine, you *are* my Old Lady." I let him get closer and closer to me, I wanted him near, I needed him. As soon as he said the word Old Lady my mind crawled out of the Blade haze and I took a step back. "Look at me. Take a good look. I'm not in leather, I'm not wearing properties. I don't belong to anyone," I went to walk past him. I wanted my boy in my arms. His hand clamped onto my forearm, halting my movements.

"You *are* mine, sugar," he stated.

I pulled my arm away from him, spun around to face him and said; "Oh yeah? Well, I hope you don't mind sharing. These guys in this club are very good to me. Very!" I winked at him and walked away from his shocked expression.

"You're letting your men have my woman?" Blade roared, looking at Mason. He stood up and walked towards us, his hands in the air, trying to calm him down.

"They have all been told that she's off limits," he said.

"Well, tell me something, *Blade.*" I made a point of calling him that as he liked me to use his real name. "Why do you get to have another woman? Why do you get to come here and claim me, yet go home to, what was her name? Oh yeah, Ashlyn?"

"Ashlyn?" Cammie piped up. "What are you doing with her? Where did she even disappear to?"

"You know her?" I asked Cammie, who was now winding Liam on her shoulder. She nodded. "I can't believe this, who is she?" I asked looking around the room at the people who obviously knew more than me.

Ring. Ring. Ring.

"Oh and what a surprise, his phone rings," I said walking away and taking my son off Cammie. "Did you know he was going to leave me too?" I saw the hurt in Cammie's eyes when I said that and I instantly regretted it.

"Heather!" Blade scolded me. "No one knew I was leaving. Hell, I didn't even know I had to go. It was all last minute."

"Why didn't you tell me?" I asked.

"I didn't know what was going on, what I was walking in to. You couldn't have come with me."

"But Ashlyn could?" Cammie asked.

"No, she disappeared the same night we rescued you both. She was there when I got there."

"Got where?" I asked again, getting frustrated.

"Family emergency, sugar."

"You told me you didn't have a family." If he kept that from me, what else had he kept from me?

"Only a sister." His phone began ringing again, he looked at the display. He wanted to answer it but I knew he didn't want to upset me more.

"Answer it," I told him. He looked into my eyes and his head bobbed in a quick nod.

"Everything ok? Hold on..." He pulled the phone away from his ear. "I gotta go. I'll be back and, sugar? You're mine. I love you." He kissed me quickly on the lips, so quick that I didn't get a chance to respond and I watched as he walked away, again. Not knowing when he was coming back.

Chapter 9

Blade

I told Heather I loved her and that I was going to be back to see her, but so many things had got in the way that it had been almost a week and I haven't been back to her. The night in the club was so fucking hot, just thinking about it makes me want to come in my boxers. I was watching her all night shake that gorgeous ass of hers, seeing her smiling and having fun was my undoing and I needed to be touching her, I couldn't stay away any longer. I never intended to stop for a drink on my way back from a run, but something was calling to me and I was over the moon to see Heather on the dance floor. I needed to come clean and tell her where I've been, what I've been doing, but I was scared that she would push me further away. I liked to think I was man enough to tell her that she was mine and have her believe me, but she was a wildcat. She would never just bow down and do everything I told her to, that was also one of the many things I loved about her. I shook my head as I laughed at myself for being so pussy whipped. I pulled into the driveway of the temporary home that I was currently living in. I looked towards the house and saw the front curtain twitching. I had responsibilities that I had to take care of, family that needed me. There was a party at the Crusaders clubhouse tomorrow night and I would be there. I climbed off my bike, pulled my helmet off my head and walked up the steps to the door. I took a deep breath and put on my happy face. I opened the door and I was greeted by a little girl hurtling towards me. I dropped my helmet and opened up my arms for her.

"You're home," she called out excitedly, her dark brown curls bouncing around.

"Yes, sweetheart, I am." I kissed her on the cheek and she giggled, my day old stubble tickling her.

"Come play with me," she wriggled so I put her on the floor and she pulled at my hand until I walked into the living room with her. She released my hand and I looked up to see Ashlyn feeding Tegan, she was only eight weeks old, dressed in pink.

"Everything ok?" I asked.

"Yeah," she said quietly. "Kelsey has been a handful today, but that's pretty normal."

"She's a typical three year old, no doubt." I rubbed my hand over my face. I had been gone for a couple of days on a run for a nearby charter that needed help. I used to love being an enforcer, but then I had no ties. Now, I had people needing me in every direction that I looked. I felt like I needed to settle down into one club, but where? "I need a shower, I bloody stink."

"He bloody stinks." Kelsey sung, laughing behind her hand as she played with her dolls on the floor.

"Kelsey." Ashlyn said in a warning tone.

"He bloody stinks. He bloody stinks. He bloody stinks," she started chanting.

"Enough!" I bellowed, I didn't have the patience for this today. I had a banging headache and all I wanted to do was sink balls deep into Heather. I needed her to be able to relax. I watched as Kelsey ran out of the room crying.

"I want Mummy," she sobbed. I looked over to Ashlyn and she was glaring at me.

"You need to be patient with her. She's only three years old for Christ sake."

"I need a shower," I grumbled, walking away and into the en-suite in my bedroom. I didn't have much stuff here, I had the clothes I needed and loneliness in my heart. I ached for Heather, my heart, body and soul needed her to function. I was incomplete without her and Liam. Seeing him a few days ago made my heart ache, I missed him so much too. I stripped out of my clothes, throwing them in the washing hamper. I climbed into the hot shower, dipped my head underneath the spray and let it run down my back and face. Heather consumed my head, my thoughts. Her body felt so amazing last week, it felt like she was going to suffocate my cock, her grip was so tight. Her walls pulsing around me, the feel of her orgasms and feeling her release run down my cock to cover my balls was almost as sexy as when she squirted all over me. I wanted to take control of her body, kiss every inch, nibble and bite her until her skin turned pink. I wanted to mark her so everyone knew that even though she wasn't wearing my properties she was in fact still mine. I worked myself over, using the shower gel to help while thoughts of Heather's sweet pussy invaded my mind. I grunted as my arousal released and I was feeling slightly calmer.

"Having fun?" I looked through the glass in the shower door to see Ashlyn standing there, watching me.

"What the hell are you doing in here?" I shouted at her.

"Calm down, we have company," she told me, passing me a towel.

"Who is it?" I grabbed the towel, wrapping it around my waist. I walked past her and into the bedroom, pulling out a clean t-shirt and putting it on. My body was still damp so the material stuck to my skin. I dropped the towel and pulled on some jeans, without boxers as I was ready to crawl into bed and sleep for a week. I didn't want much to get in the way of that.

"Um… CG?" she said it like she was asking me. This woman frustrated me to no end. I walked out of the room to see CG pacing in the hall way. When he heard me he stopped and looked up at me.

"Hey, man," he smiled.

"How did you find me?" I asked, not exchanging pleasantries.

I didn't want anyone knowing about my shit until I had spoken to Heather. I just needed to find the right way and time to tell her. If CG knew about me then I'm guessing I needed to tell Heather pretty quick.

"It doesn't take much, once I set myself on a job I get it done."

"Job? Uno sent you?" I asked crossing my arms across my chest and widening my stance.

"Na, it's just me. Need your help." I nodded my head for him to continue and he looked behind me. I looked over my shoulder to see Ashlyn standing there with Tegan in her arms.

"Give us a minute," I told her. She nodded and I saw her head in the direction of the girls' bedroom.

"Got a nice little set up here, haven't you?" he chuckled.

"Shut it and tell me what you want." I walked past him and into the living room, I had to step over all the dolls and girly shit that was covering the floor.

"We need you back at the club, man," he said looking at me. "Since Dad found out about Liam, him not being who he thought he was, he's kinda gone off the rails. Drinking more, taking drugs. I even saw him with a sweet bun the other day."

"Shit," I cursed. One thing that Uno never done was sleep around, he loved Gloria and in all the time I've known them he was faithful.

"He's got sloppy too, we got invaded by the Satan MC..."

"Wait, I thought we killed them all?" I cut him off.

"They were in Satan cuts. Must have missed some." He shrugged his shoulders. "Dad's shot was off and he ended up shooting Riz in the shoulder."

"Fuck!" I dropped my head in my hands. If I needed to go back then I wanted Heather with me, which means I have to grow a pair and tell her why I had to leave.

"So, you coming back?" he asked, looking hopeful, though I don't know what he thought I'd be able to do.

"I need to talk to Heather first."

"Yeah, what the hell is going on here? You got a built in

family?"

"None of your business. I'll talk to you soon." I stood up and waited until he left the room and I heard the front door slam shut. I sat back down and tried to form a plan of what I was going to do in my head. I heard little footsteps and looked up when Kelsey ran into the room. She stopped when she saw me.

"Come here, sweetheart," I told her, holding my hand out to her. She took it and I pulled her into my lap. "I didn't mean to upset you earlier, I'm sorry."

"That's ok," she quietly said, resting her head on my shoulder. We stayed like that for a few minutes, after I realised she wasn't going to move I sunk back into the sofa and got comfy. My eyes were getting heavy, I had been on my bike for a solid ten hours and needed to sleep. I heard some movements and I opened my eyes. Ashlyn handed me Tegan, she was asleep and I placed her on my chest. I looked over to Kelsey who was also asleep with her thumb in her mouth.

"I gotta get some shopping done." Ashlyn said as she looked through her bag and pulled out her car keys.

"Sweetheart, I've been riding for hours. I need some sleep," I told her, yawning.

"They're your responsibility, Blade. They're both tired, put them to bed," she told me.

"Ashlyn, please." I pleaded before she walked out of the door and I heard the front door close. I held on tight to both girls as I climbed to my feet, walking towards the room that they shared. It had a bed for Kelsey and Tegan's cot was in here for her to sleep in during the day, at night time she was in a moses basket in my room. I got both girls changed and into bed within thirty minutes and once my head hit the pillow I was out for the count.

Chapter 10

Heather

My emotions had been all over the place for the last week. Cammie had explained how she knew Ashlyn, but we couldn't figure out why Blade was with her. Cammie was convinced he wasn't cheating on me but I just didn't know. I wanted to be mad at Blade for leaving me, but when I was around him all I wanted to feel was his arms around me, his breath on my neck and his heart beating in time with mine. When we were together we were one.

"You ready?" Cammie asked as she poked her head in around the door. We no longer shared a room, she spent nearly all of her time with Mason now and it seemed silly for her to come back here to get clean clothes.

"I'm just waiting on Penny to come and look after him." I nodded my head towards a sleeping Liam.

"I'm here," she called out as she walked into the room carrying her laptop and food.

"Why aren't you working tonight?" Cammie asked her.

"You may be sleeping with the VP but he hasn't claimed you as an Old Lady so you can't question me." Penny snapped at her. I saw that Cammie wanted to argue back, her mouth was opening and closing like a fish but no words were coming out.

"He's been changed and fed, so he should sleep. Any problems come and find me."

"No problem." She settled herself onto what was Cammie's bed and started up her laptop. I linked arms with Cammie and we walked into the bar which was overflowing with people. We walked up to the bar and before we could ask

Drake, the prospect passed us two glasses of wine. We smiled at him and walked around to find a place to sit.

"What was up with Penny earlier?" Cammie asked as she pointed at an empty table.

Once we were sitting, I told her, "She has an infection, so she can't work."

"Oh." Cammie laughed. "I bet she's hating that."

"What's so funny over here?" Mason asked as he and Solar sat down with us. Mason kissed me on the cheek and kissed Cammie a little more forcefully on the lips. I felt like I was invading on a private moment so I turned in my seat to look at Solar.

"You ok? Haven't seen you around much."

"Yeah, just busy, you know…"

"Club business," I cut him off, knowing exactly what he was going to come out with. "So, what's this party for?"

"It's just a Friday night, babe," he chuckled. It was full of people, the bar was crazy busy and Lottie was helping to serve.

"Oh, I love this song. Wanna dance?" I asked him. He smiled, grabbed my hand and led me onto the dance floor. He pulled me close to him and started moving his hips from side to side, making me giggle. He spun me around and pulled me up close to his chest and he started moving his hips seductively. I could feel his arousal, there was no use in me getting excited as I knew that none of these guys would take it any further. Apparently once you are claimed as an Old Lady no one wants to get in the middle of that. Did I want that? No, I was in love with Blade, I only wanted him.

We had been dancing to a few songs when I felt him disappear from behind me, I turned around and saw a pissed off Blade looking at me. I didn't move as he prowled closer towards me.

"What do you think you're doing?" he growled against my ear so I could hear him.

"Dancing," I replied.

"Don't get smart with me, sugar. Else I'll show you who you belong to."

"Doesn't sound much like a threat," I purred pushing my body up against his. His hands found my hips and held them tightly. I looked up at him under my eyelashes and licked my lips.

"Hmm, you're gonna be the death of me, woman," he slammed his lips down onto mine and I finally relaxed, I felt complete. We stayed where we were, in the middle of the dance floor dancing and kissing, "I love you, sugar."

"I love you too." I smiled.

"We need to talk. Where's Liam?"

"Penny is looking after him in my room," he nodded and led me off the dance floor and away from the noise, it was much quieter outside.

"Let's sit over there." He nodded to a picnic bench and we sat next to each other. I was patiently waiting for him to start talking.

"Blade," I said after we sat in silence for what felt like hours but in reality was only a few minutes.

"Kade," he reminded me, "I want you to call me Kade."

"Ok." I nodded.

"The only family I have…" He stopped talking and cleared his throat. "Had left, was my sister."

"What do you mean had?"

"She died six weeks ago. Cancer."

"Oh, Kade. I'm so sorry." I wrapped my arms around him and held on to him tightly.

"She's the reason I had to go. I…"

"BLADE!" A woman called out, when I looked over to where the voice had come from I saw a small, blonde woman carrying a baby in one arm and dragging a toddler by the hand, who was having trouble keeping up with her fast pace.

"Ashlyn," he said leaving me and hurrying towards her.

"What's happened? What are you doing here?"

"Kade?" I asked, standing behind him. Wondering what the hell was going on and whose kids they were.

"We had to hide…" She looked scared, she was trembling and her breath was uneven.

"Here, give her to me." He took the baby from her arms. "Sugar, this is Tegan. Can you hold her for a minute?" I nodded and took the little girl bundled up in a pink blanket. She was adorable, blue eyes staring at me and a scattering of dark hair on her head. I felt my body crumble slightly at the thought that I'd never have a daughter.

"Why did you have to hide? Kelsey, sweetheart, come here." Blade held out his arms and the other little girl walked towards him. He picked her up and held her against his chest. She placed her chin on his shoulder and smiled at me. I tickled her cheek and she giggled.

"I don't know who they were. I heard a bike and thought it was you. But I remembered you saying you wouldn't be back tonight. I looked out the window and it was a load of bikes. I didn't know what to do. I grabbed the girls and we hid in the garden. I could hear them trashing the house."

"Who were they? The guy that came over yesterday?" He placed his palm on the side of her face, getting her to look at him. I felt a surge of jealousy rip through my body. I didn't want him touching anyone else. Was it an intimate touch? Were these his daughters?

"No, these guys were older."

"In leather jackets?" She nodded. "What did they look like?"

"I… I don't remember. I think it was red, a devil or something."

"Satan," he mumbled quietly.

"What? The Satan MC? Have they come back looking for me? I thought they were dead? I saw you kill them," she was panicking and starting to hyperventilate. "You burned it down," she whispered, tears running down her face. Blade held her close to him and Kelsey as she cried.

"Kade, let's go inside," I told him. He looked at me and nodded. We walked down the dark hallway and into my bedroom.

"Heather, you're back early?" Penny said, looking up from her laptop.

"Thanks for watching him, everything ok?" I asked as I walked over to check on him and still holding Tegan in my arms.

"Yeah, fine. Who are they?"

"None of your business, out!" Blade demanded. She looked him over, recognising his cut and left the room, quickly. Ashlyn stood in the middle of the room shaking, Blade placed Kelsey on my bed and she curled up against my pillow, sucking her thumb. Her eyes looking heavy.

"What's going on?" I asked, sitting on Cammie's bed and rocking Tegan as she began to cry, which set Liam off and he started to cry too. I looked over to him and watched as Blade walked over to him and picked him up. He quietened instantly and I saw the love Blade had for him in his eyes.

"Are these your daughters?" I asked Blade. Ashlyn looked towards him surprised.

"I thought you was going to tell her?" she said.

"I haven't had a chance yet. No, sugar. They're my nieces." He sat next to me on the bed. "When my sister found out she had cancer she was already pregnant with Tegan. She refused treatment and refused to have an abortion. Once Tegan was born, they discovered the cancer was too aggressive and nothing could be done." Blade was getting choked up and I placed my hand on his face as a way of comfort, normally I would have climbed into his lap, but that would have been difficult with the two babies between us. "The night I left, I got a call from Ashlyn, telling me to hurry, telling me that my sister wouldn't be with us much longer. I didn't have time to stop and explain. I had to get to her to say goodbye, I didn't want to miss the chance. I told Uno I was going and left. No explanations to anyone. I am so sorry I left the way I did. But she was my sister." A few stray tears fell down his face and I reached up to wipe them away.

"I'll give you two some privacy." Ashlyn said.

"Thank you," I said. "Cammie's in the bar. She'll keep you company." She nodded and walked out of the door. I stood up and placed Tegan in Liam's moses basket, then I took Liam from Blade and put him in there with her. I was surprised they both fit, with Liam being much bigger than her. I walked back to Blade and pulled him close to me. I stood in between his open legs and his head fell against my stomach. His tears soaking my top. After a few minutes, Blade pulled back and he looked more composed.

"Where does Ashlyn fit into all of this? Is she your..."

"She was my sister's best friend. She came to the Devon clubhouse to tell me about her stubbornness. Hoping that I could get her to change her mind. That's when the Satan's grabbed her. They came back for Cammie once they discovered I had never met her. They used her as a play toy."

"Oh God," I gasped, covering my mouth with my hand.

"She was there for months. She's been helping me with them. But I can't expect her to help forever. I want them to grow up having a mum," he pointed at me, "And a dad," he pointed to himself.

"Oh."

"You don't want that?"

"Oh, Kade. Of course I want that. Of course I'll help you. Does that mean moving back to Devon?" I asked, disappointed in the fact. I loved Cornwall and wanted to stay here.

"I'm not sure." He explained the visit he had from Neil and now with the Satan's apparently being around again, no one was safe. A lockdown may need to be called, for the Crusaders and the Destroyers. "Now, are you mine?" he asked. I nodded.

"I've always been yours," I whispered.

"That's what I like to hear. I want to see that property back on that gorgeous body of yours."

"Uno took it from me," I told him.

"What?" he shouted, standing up. I winced as I thought all the children would wake up but they didn't.

"He told me I had to give it back. I was no longer an Old Lady and you had gone enforcer. That I could stay if I worked for them, or stay in your house but I had to pay him rent."

"That cheeky fucker," he growled. "I never asked for it back. To me, you will always be my Old Lady. You could have stayed in our home, it's ours and has nothing to do with that club." I nodded, that was always good to know, for the future.

"Come on, sugar. Let's get some sleep before I talk to these guys about the Satan's."

"We can't leave them in there together. I'll go and find Carla, see if she has a cot we can borrow."

"I'll come with you," he said, standing up.

"Babe, you need to stay with them. What if Kelsey wakes up?" He nodded and I hurried to find Carla.

Blade

It felt good getting everything off my chest, telling Heather about my sister. I was relieved when she agreed to help me raise the girls, we would have the large family she wanted and if she wanted more we would adopt. I heard a noise outside of the door and opened it to see what was going on. There was the Prez, VP and Tat carrying a cot down the hall and figuring out how to get it through the door. Behind them was Heather, Ashlyn and Cammie. Once the cot was in the room, I heard Kelsey.

"Uncle Kade?" She was sucking her thumb and rubbing her

eyes. I saw out of the corner of my eye that Heather and Ashlyn both went to go to her at the same time, when they noticed what they both done, they stopped, telling each other to go to her.

"It's ok, she doesn't know me." Heather told Ashlyn. "You go." I could see how much Heather wanted to comfort her. She busied herself with making the cot comfy for the babies. Cammie and Heather changed the babies and put them to sleep in the cot that was borrowed from the Prez's wife. I pulled the guys to the side.

"I know this isn't my club, but we need a church meeting in the morning, early. It's important."

"You got it." Prez said, slapping me on the back. "See you at six am." I nodded my appreciation.

"There's a bed next door for you." Cammie told Ashlyn.

"Shall I take her with me?" Ashlyn asked, talking about Kelsey, I nodded. I needed some time alone with my woman before all hell broke loose. Especially if that meant calling a lockdown.

Once Ashlyn left, I pushed the two single beds together, there was no way I was going to sleep separate from my woman tonight. I pulled her close to me and began removing her jeans.

"I just want to feel your skin tonight," I whispered to her.

"I want that too, but I can't. Not yet."

"Why?" She stepped back and pulled her top off over her head and undid her bra, letting it fall down her arms. "What are those? Who did that? Who had their hands on my woman's breasts?" I growled, trying not to shout. I didn't want to wake up Liam and Tegan.

"You can't touch them. They're still healing. I have to wear a bra to bed so I don't get them caught in the bed sheets," she explained, pulling her bra back on.

"Fine, but you're only wearing a bra," I told her. She nodded. "Holes?"

"Yes, Mason did them, and this?" She stuck her tongue out and I lunged for her, causing us to collapse on the bed. I kissed her hard and she forced her tongue into my mouth, I couldn't wait to feel that all over my cock.

"I'm not happy that he got to touch you."

"He's seen it all before," she said, like it was no big deal.

"Not helping, sugar," I grumbled. "Besides, you were a girl then. Now you're a woman. My woman."

"Yes, I am. All yours." She kissed me again and we crawled into bed.

"I love you, sugar."

"I love you too."

Chapter 11

Blade

"Why the fuck are we up so early?" Solar complained as we all walked into the room that church was held in. We all sat around the large glass table, I held back and let the guys all take their usual seats and I sat where there was an empty one. "Right, Blade called this meeting, so go ahead, son, tell us what's going on." Prez said.

"My family were invaded by the Satan MC last night, the Devon Destroyers clubhouse was also targeted." I didn't know how much these guys knew.

"We haven't had any trouble with them before." Holes said.

"They have a problem with me, they killed my wife and daughter a couple of years ago and I got my revenge by killing their Prez and VP."

"Holy shit!" Solar exclaimed.

"They started a feud with Devon Destroyers, a turf war, and all hell broke loose when they took something that was ours... I don't wanna bring you guys danger, but it's not safe for Heather or Cammie to be out there."

"Lockdown?" Tat asked, looking at the Prez.

"Blade?" Prez asked me.

"I think for safety, it might be a good idea."

"Ok, all families are to be here within the hour. Anything else?"

"Prez." Toes said, looking up from his laptop. "I got it, the location of the building the pigs are looking for."

"Well?" VP asked.

"It's not far from here." He began explaining where it was and why they needed to go there.

"Blade, you wanna ride with us?" Prez asked.

"What about the girls?" Who were going to protect them if we were out on a run?

"We'll leave Drake and Jase here with them. They're good prospects." I nodded my head in agreement. "We'll leave tonight." He slammed the gavel down and everyone stood up and left the room. I headed back towards Heather's room, I left her fast asleep this morning but wanted to get back as Tegan was an early riser. As I walked back into the room, I heard Tegan fussing. I scooped her out of the cot and ran my hand over the top of Liam's head to lure him back to sleep.

"Kade?" I heard Heather mumble sleepily. I looked towards her as she sat herself up in bed.

"Morning, sugar." I walked towards her and dipped my head to give her a kiss. She held out her arms and I passed Tegan over to her.

"How old is she?"

"Eight weeks."

"Oh God and so young to lose a mum. Did you get there in time, to say goodbye?" I nodded my head as I sat on the bed beside them and looked into Tegan's bright eyes. "What are we going to do? Where are we going?"

"We're staying put here for a minute, sugar… There's a lockdown."

"Oh, are we in danger?" She looked panicked.

"Sugar, I will never let anything happen to you and our kids. You're safe." She nodded and we sat there quietly while Tegan was content playing with her own hands.

Knock. Knock. Knock.

"Uncle Kade!" Kelsey called out, not waiting for an answer and pushing the door open. I threw a t-shirt at Heather before she bounded in, curls bouncing around her shoulders and she jumped up onto the bed in front of us.

"Morning, sweetheart." I leant forward and gave her a kiss on the cheek and she climbed into my lap, leaning over and kissing Tegan on the head. She looked at Heather as if she wanted to say something.

"Are you going to be my new mummy now? Uncle Kade is going to be my daddy, as we live with him, I've never had a daddy before. My mummy is with the angels now." She pointed towards the sky as she told us that. Heather looked at me, unsure what to tell her, I shrugged my shoulders, I didn't know much about kids either.

"I'm not going to be your new mummy, I'll be an extra mummy, as your mummy still loves you very much and she's watching over you every day." Liam let out a small wail and Heather looked over to him.

"I'll get him," I walked over and picked Liam up. I held him against my chest and he calmed down. Kelsey was watching my every movement.

"Is that baby ours too?" She looked happy at the thought.

"Yes, sweetheart. This is Liam." She looked at him and gave him a kiss on the head like she did with Tegan.

"I'm a big sister to two babies?" She asked holding up two fingers.

"Yes, sweetheart." She nodded her head and looked between them.

"I'm hungry."

"Let's go and get you some food. Where's Ashlyn?" I asked her as I balanced both babies in my arms so Heather could get herself ready.

"Sleeping."

We all made our way into the clubhouse dining room and the Prez's wife, Carla, was already up and cooking. She made some toast for Kelsey and I watched over her with Liam as Heather made the bottles up for the babies.

***

The Prez made a few of his guys do a swap of rooms, so we

were now in a large room with a double bed and a single one and still had plenty of room for the cot. We were keeping the babies in together until we had some time to go and buy new ones. We would never fit two cots in this room.

"You gonna be ok, sugar?" I asked her as she was sitting on the bed with Tegan and Liam laid out in front of her, she was tickling them, trying to get them both to smile. It was easy with Liam, he was always happy. "Cammie and Ashlyn are here to help."

"I don't need help. I can do this. I want to be able to look after them, I don't want someone always with us."

"Just call if they get too much." She nodded. I kissed her on the lips briefly before looking at Kelsey who was sitting on her bed playing with her dolls. Holes and I made a trip to where we were staying, grabbing as much stuff as we could, mainly clothes and toys. If it was in fact the Satan MC that invaded my home they sure did a good job, they completely trashed the place.

"Bye, sweetheart," I said to Kelsey, giving her a kiss on the top of her head.

"Bye, Daddy," she said not looking up at me. My head snapped to look at Heather and she was smiling at me. I wasn't going to make a big deal out of it. I kissed Liam and Tegan on their heads and Heather once more before I turned around and met up with everyone else to check out this warehouse that Toes had found.

***

Prez, VP, Tat, Toes, Solar and myself all left our bikes at the top of the hill, we could see the warehouse but we didn't want to alert anyone that we were here. We were here mainly to find out who was behind this sex trafficking business that the police were unable to find.

Once we were closer to the building we hid in groups of two,

Prez and Toes were behind a large van, Tat and Solar were behind a shed and me and VP were tucked away behind some large bins.

"The door's opening." VP said as he made a hand signal telling everyone not to move. We all stayed quiet until we could see who it was.

"Shit," I cursed.

"What is it?" VP whispered.

"That's the Satan MC."

"So?"

"They're the ones that kidnapped your girl."

"What the fuck?" he growled. Maybe that wasn't the best time to tell him that, would he be on a revenge mission now? "She was kidnapped? When did this happen?"

"Fuck, did you not know?" He shook his head, "Sorry, man."

"Let's get these fuckers." He pulled the safety off his gun and I grabbed his arm.

"These guys mean business, they will kill us all," I told him.

"They will get what's coming to them, no one takes my girl and gets away with it." VP motioned his hand to let them all know he was going in. I followed him closely behind, Heather would never forgive me if I let anything happen to him. It was strangely quiet and it had me thinking we were walking into a trap. As we walked closer to the main doors I heard movement and pulled Holes so we weren't directly in front of the door. One man walked out alone and I grabbed him by the head, covered his mouth and threatened him with my knife at his throat. I walked back so he was against the house and I was in his personal space.

"How many of you are there?" I demanded.

"Fuck you," he spat in my face. I dug the knife in harder and I heard him whimper when blood started oozing from him.

"Wanna try again?" I asked. I looked over and saw Holes was keeping a constant look out, I didn't know where the other brothers had gone.

"Four... Only four," he admitted.

"Good." I looked over and saw Holes watching us, I knew what he wanted so I stepped aside and let him deal with him. He didn't hesitate, he shot him in the chest. "Fuck, they would have heard that," I cursed.

"Don't care, I'm going in." He turned around and kicked the door in, shooting as soon as he saw anyone. One guy was dead inside on the dirty concrete floor. I could hear a struggle going on further into the house, I stepped over the large bearded man and pushed a door open that led to an even dirtier kitchen area. Paint peeling off the walls, dirt and dried blood covering the floors. It was disgusting, I heard a gunshot and the roar of bikes. I ran outside and was shocked at what I saw. Riding away was two bikes, both in Devon Destroyers jackets.

"Blade, we need to find the girls," I looked over my shoulder and saw Toes looking at me. I nodded my head and followed him into the house. I saw a dead body at the bottom of the stairs. "There may be more. VP said there were four and we've only killed two."

"I saw two riding away," I told him. He nodded but we kept our weapons out in case there were any more people about. We walked up the stairs, I followed behind Toes making sure no one could sneak up behind us. Once we reached the top of the stairs there were two doors, Toes opened the first one and it was an empty bathroom. We moved on to the next door and it was locked. He looked at me and I nodded my head in agreement that we should kick it in. He took a step back and slammed his foot into the door. Toes was a large guy, bulging muscles, covered in tattoos. Screams erupted in the room and we hurried in, I stopped dead in my tracks when I looked into the dark and damp room. The room was covered in mattresses and ten different aged women were all huddled together in one corner of the room.

"Prez." Toes shouted down the stairs and within a couple of

minutes the rest of the guys were standing in the room too.
"Get Drake here with the van." Prez demanded.
"What about the girls and families?" Solar asked.
"You and Blade head back there and we'll get this place
cleared up. We don't want anyone finding it, Brett told us this
place existed, if he finds it like this he'll know we had
something to do with it," he explained. I nodded and as me
and Solar left the room I could hear Holes trying to talk to the
girls, he was probably the least scary looking out of them all. I
rushed to my bike, in a hurry to get back to my family. As I
was about to pull my helmet on I saw Holes running towards
his bike. He climbed on and took off with Solar and myself not
far behind him.

Chapter 12

Heather

Carla had been a great help, she had dug out all of her old stuff she used when her kids were little. She found a playpen the babies could sleep in and her daughter Olivia, who was four, kept Kelsey amused. They were sitting at a table with Danny who was two and they were finger painting. Ashlyn was trying to take a step back and let me care for them as I was going to be looking after them in the future. I didn't want her to feel pushed out. She was staring into space, looking out the side window in the clubhouse.

"You ok?" I asked as I moved to sit beside her on the worn out leather sofa.

"Yeah," she sighed.

"You sure about that?" I didn't want to pry but I didn't want her feeling like she couldn't talk to me either.

"She was my best friend, you know?" She paused and I kept quiet. "She was always there for me and now I have no one. I hated that I was away from her for those couple of months. She went downhill fast."

"That must have been scary for you being at the Satan clubhouse?" I asked.

"Yeah, I've never met a group of guys that are so scary and that liked to inflict pain." She paused and took a deep breath. I saw something change in her eyes. "Anyway you don't want to hear about that."

"I'm here if you ever need to talk. You're not alone, not anymore." She smiled and I wanted to give her a hug but hesitated.

"Thank you."

"Mummy, look what I made." I looked up and Kelsey was waving me over. I smiled at Ashlyn and walked over to inspect her art work. I was a bit overwhelmed that she had called me mummy, I knew kids adapted well but it still shocked me. I spoke to Carla and she explained that it could be a coping mechanism for her, as she wanted to be the same as the babies because we called me and Blade mummy and daddy in front of them.

"That looks great, sweetie," I said as I knelt down beside her and inspected her painting. There was a whole load of noise and I looked up to see a furious looking Mason walking in through the doors, his eyes scanned the room and once they settled on Cammie, they softened.

"Cammie, bedroom. NOW!" he demanded. She nodded and made her way towards him, once she was close enough he reached for her hand and dragged her towards the bedrooms. My eyes kept looking at the door, waiting for Blade to come back. I hated the thought that something may happen to him. A few seconds later he walked in and I stood up and rushed towards him, throwing my arms around him and burying my head in his neck. He was taller than me so I had to stretch up on tip toes to reach him.

"Hey, you ok?" he asked, rubbing my back. I nodded my head but didn't break apart from him. I hated that we spent so many weeks apart, it was one of the worst times in my life and I never wanted to be separated from him again. I pulled back and cupped my hand around the back of his neck to pull his head towards me so I could claim his lips. Just as our lips barely touched, Liam let out a wail which woke Tegan up and she started crying too.

"Mummy, the babies are crying!" Kelsey called out. I pulled away from Blade and walked over to the play pen and pulled Liam out. He was having a major tantrum, his face was red and his fists were clenched together tightly.

"Sugar, give him here." Blade said as he walked towards me. "Go to daddy," I told Liam. Blade took him from me and walked over to the leather sofa where Ashlyn was sitting. He flicked the TV on and cradled Liam in his arms, rocking him gently. Within a couple of minutes he was quiet. I had managed to calm Tegan down as soon as I picked her up. I looked at the clock and saw that it was nearly noon.

"I'll get their bottles made," I said to Blade and he nodded. "Kelsey you want a sandwich for lunch?" I asked her. She shook her head.

"Crackers and cheese please," she smiled at me.

"I'll see what I can find." I ran my hand over her head and she swatted my hand away. As I walked towards the kitchen I saw Cammie leaving Mason's room alone. She looked up at me and her eyes were watery. I stopped walking and waited for her to come closer. "You ok?"

"Yes," she smiled.

"You're smiling?" I asked confused.

"Yeah," she nodded.

"Ok, I'm confused. You look like you've been crying."

"I have," she hesitated, looking around. "Mason asked me to be his Old Lady," she smiled.

"Really?"

"Why do you looked so surprised? I know I'm not good enough for him. I mean, I've got baggage, I'm a club whore," she looked down to the ground when she said that.

"No," I told her.

"I *do not* want to hear you saying that again," Mason bellowed behind us. We both spun around and he had his hands fisted at his sides, legs spread wide and an angry look on his face. He walked slowly towards us and once he reached Cammie he put his finger under her chin so she would look at him, "You are *not* a club whore. You are my Old Lady. Got it?"

"I haven't said yes yet," she softly said which earnt a growl from Mason and a chuckle from me.

"You will," he pecked her on the lips before he walked away. We both waited until he was around the corner until we both burst into giggles.

"Did you see the look on his face?" I said.

"Yep, he is determined." Cammie laughed.

"Why didn't you say yes? You want to be his Old Lady, I know you do," I pushed the kitchen door open and once we were both inside I passed Tegan to Cammie and sorted out making some lunch.

"Yeah, I do. It's just…" She hesitated, "Don't you think it's a bit quick?"

"Don't talk to me about things being quick. I hadn't known Kade for ten minutes before he was claiming me and yesterday morning I had one son and now I have two daughters as well."

"You were born to be a mum, Heather. Look at you, you practically have twins. One's just five weeks older than the other," she laughed.

"Mummy!" Kelsey called out as she pushed the kitchen door open, "I'm hungry. You're taking foreber," she exclaimed, not pronouncing her words right and placing her hands on her hips.

"It's coming. Sit at the breakfast bar with auntie Cammie while I finish it," I told her and Cammie helped her sit on the stool.

"Kelsey!" Blade barked as he walked into the room with Liam in his arms. "What have I told you about running away from me?"

"Not to do it," she quietly said as her head dipped and her bottom lip trembled. "But I…"

"No buts," he cut her off.

"I'm sorry," she said. "I won't do it again, Daddy," she smiled at him and I saw him soften before my very eyes. He couldn't be mad at her when she looked so cute and when she called him daddy.

"Us guys have got to stick together," he said to Liam as I passed him a bottle and he walked out of the room.

***

We had an uneventful day, I tried my best to keep Kelsey entertained. It was difficult trying to explain to her why we couldn't just leave and go to the park or the beach. Blade said it wasn't safe for her to even play outside for the minute, not until they knew what was going on, of course I asked what he meant and got the usual reply of 'Club business'.

We had put the babies to bed and I was reading Kelsey a story while Blade showered. Considering we didn't have an overly active day, she was out like a light. I walked in to the bathroom hoping that Blade hadn't finished yet so I could join him. I was surprised when I walked in and he was sitting on the closed toilet seat, his head in his hands.

"You ok?" I asked as I walked closer towards him. He couldn't have heard me walk in as he jumped when I spoke.

"Oh, yeah. Just thinking." He rubbed his hand over his face, stood up and slipped off his jacket then pulled his t-shirt over his head.

"Oh yeah, about what?" I asked. He lowered his head so his lips were touching my ear.

"Club business, sugar." He kissed that spot below my ear and my body trembled. We had only been back together officially for two days and apart from that one time in the club a week ago, we hadn't had much contact apart from kisses. My body needed him, every time he was near, my skin heated and my core pulsed. He pulled my t-shirt off over my head and unsnapped my bra. As it fell away his hands were kneading my breasts and his head dipped and he ran his tongue over one of my piercings. I stepped back and shook my head, they weren't fully healed yet and I didn't want them to get infected.

"You can do an additional solution treatment on them later. I'm not keeping my tongue and lips away from them any longer." He pulled at my leggings until they were around my ankles. He grabbed my hips and placed me onto the sink, I balanced on the edge as he pulled my leggings and flip flops off my feet. I stretched out with my foot and placed it on the bath tub directly opposite us so I wouldn't fall. I opened my legs the best I could when Blade stood in between them.

"You are so fucking sexy," he whispered into my ear. My body trembled, my nipples hardened and my skin was covered in goose bumps. He lowered his head and I raised mine ready to kiss him when he bypassed my lips and went straight for my nipples. He brushed his lips over the tips and I loved the sensation of feeling his soft lips and then the roughness of stubble on them. His tongue darted out of his mouth and he licked and nibbled on them, my head fell back from the pleasure and I moaned. He chuckled and the vibration shot straight through my core. While he was distracted, I pulled at his belt until it loosened and flicked the button open on his jeans. I pushed my hand inside and grabbed hold of him, he moaned which caused another vibration to shoot over my body. I used my leg that wasn't holding me up to push his jeans down.

"Can you be quiet, sugar?" he asked, looking at me and I frantically nodded. I'd bite a hole in my lip if I had to, all I wanted was for him to be inside of me. He pulled at my legs so I would wrap them around him as he picked me up and walked towards the wall next to the bathroom door. He always favoured a wall over everything else.

"Babe, we can't," I panted. He pulled back to look at me, confusion on his face. "The wall will be too noisy. Kelsey will definitely wake up." He groaned and moved me. He shuffled towards the side unit, his jeans still around his ankles. Once I was sitting on the unit he kicked his jeans off and pulled my hips so I was hanging off the edge and he dropped to his knees. He pushed my legs further apart and he looked at me, eyes full of hunger and desire. I rose my hips in the air slightly telling him to stop teasing me. He scratched the inside of my thighs with his whiskers and I felt myself dampen even more. "Kade, please," I begged.

"That's it, sugar. That's all I wanted," he chuckled before kissing the inside of my thighs and running his tongue over my wet lips. He focused on my clit, sucking and nipping until I was writhing in pleasure. My hands were behind me, keeping me in a sitting position, my head was slung back and my hair was tickling my bare skin. I bit down on my lip and Blade pushed two fingers inside of me and began rubbing against my g-spot. I wanted to cry out from the pleasure but knew that I couldn't. Once by body stopped convulsing and my breathing was almost back to normal, I looked at Kade. "Did you lock the door?"

"Yeah, the bathroom door is locked." He fisted his cock and pumped it a couple of times.

"I meant the bedroom door, in case Kelsey wakes up."

"Yes, sugar. It's locked." He grabbed the back of my head and pulled me closer, claiming my lips roughly. I let out a little yelp and he chuckled. I wrapped my arms around his broad shoulders and he pulled me off the side unit and straight onto his hard cock. I gasped in surprise as I wasn't expecting it. "I want to be pounding you into a wall but, as I can't, I'll settle for impaling you onto my cock."

"Yes!" I called out. He positioned us so my thighs were resting on top of his forearms with his arms under my legs holding onto my bum. He pulled and pushed me with all of his strength and I couldn't do anything but hold on for the ride. I wrapped my arms around his neck and kissed and nibbled at his skin that I could reach. I could feel my orgasm approaching and as my walls tightened I could feel him grow and knew I was about to scream. I dipped my head into his neck and bit down to muffle my cries of pleasure. He groaned and I wasn't sure if it was his release making him groan or me biting him. Maybe it was both. After a couple minutes, he pulled me off him and placed me on my feet, my legs were like jelly and I flopped down onto the closed toilet seat.

"You bit me," he complained as he studied the mark in the mirror.

"It wasn't that hard. I didn't draw blood." I stood up and walked over to him. I wrapped my arms around his waist, placed my head on his back and felt my eyes closing. When he tried to move my eyes snapped open.

"Come on sugar, we need to shower." I nodded and let him pick me up and carry me into the shower. I had a lot of restless night's sleep while he was away from us and I felt like it was all of a sudden catching up on me.

We showered quickly, washing our bodies. I tried to keep my hair as much out of the water as possible. I didn't want to have to dry that now.

"Don't forget to clean those properly," he said pointing at my breasts as he climbed out of the shower.

"Can you pass me the solution?" I asked pointing to the bottle on the side of the sink. He nodded and passed it to me before wrapping a towel around his waist.

"I'll meet you in bed." He winked at me. I smiled at him and blew him a kiss. I couldn't erase the smile off my face even if I wanted to. I was happy, I had my man back and we were a family, a bigger family of five.

Chapter 13

Blade

There had been no sign of trouble over the last several weeks, no news of sex trafficking, no invasions and no sign of the Satan MC. We had been patrolling constantly over the last few weeks, I had made the trip a couple of times with Drake up to the Satan clubhouse and it was still as burnt down as ever. If they had set up somewhere else we hadn't heard of it. I had spoken to a few other MC's and no one has seen any trace of them.

"Hey, can you change her please?" Heather asked as she passed me Tegan along with an outfit. I took her over to the changing table and started cleaning her up, I had to make sure I used the right size nappies as Liam was in bigger ones than her.

"What is this?" I asked, holding up the pink frilly dress that Heather had given me.

"It's her outfit for today. Or until she makes a mess on it."

"I'd definitely throw up on this if I was you, little lady," I whispered to her, which earnt me a gurgle and lots of arms and legs flying around.

"Right, I need a shower…" Heather started telling me when there was a knock on the door, I checked to make sure she was covered up first before I opened it. I stood in the doorway with Tegan in my arms, Tat was standing in front of me and Tegan started crying. She was going through a stage of not liking other people at the minute. Heather took her out of my arms and passed me Liam instead.

"Hey, little dude." Tat said to him, which earnt him a big

smile. I passed Liam to Tat, he was a sociable little baby and all the guys loved him.

"What's up?" I asked him, leaning on the doorframe.

"Oh, I got distracted. The pigs are here, they wanna see you, man."

"What do the police want with me?" I asked quietly so Heather didn't hear.

"Don't know. Come on." He nodded his head and began walking away, still carrying Liam.

"Sugar, I got a meeting. Won't be long." I blew her a kiss and winked at Kelsey who was watching cartoons.

"Kade, you're meant to be helping me. Where's Liam?" she asked, placing her hands on her curvy hips. I wanted to place my hands on her hips and pull her up close to my body. I shook my head and cleared my throat.

"Tat's got him. I gotta go. Club…"

"Business, yeah I know. Go on, go." She shooed me away and I blew her a kiss and told her that I loved her.

I walked down the brightly lit hallway and into the bar area where I saw Prez, VP and the rest of the members sitting and standing, along with a policeman.

"Blade." Prez said, nodding his head to a seat.

"Boss." I nodded my head at him and sat down, looking around for Tat, he was sitting on the sofa bouncing Liam on his knee. "Sorry, I didn't realise you were waiting for me, you could have started, I would have caught up."

"This is about you, son," Prez said to me. "This is Brett. He's a good guy, we can trust him."

I looked at the guy, he was well built, clean shaven, with brown hair and brown eyes. He was watching me and I wondered what the hell was going on.

"Blade, we need your help." Brett said.

"Who does? The police? What the hell do they need me for?" I was sitting casually in my chair looking at him. He wasn't intimidated by any of us not like most people were.

"Yeah, we need you to go back to the Devon Destroyers. We need info…"

"You want me to rat? No way, man. No way, I ain't no rat." I pushed my chair out and stood to my feet.

"Blade." Prez said in a warning tone. I didn't leave, I started pacing in front of where Brett was sitting. I ran my hands over my short hair and down my face.

"Something fishy is going on, we need to know what." Brett told me.

"Why do you need to know? Surely it's Devon police that deal with them?" I asked.

"Usually, but they have been here a few times doing business. I think they have another warehouse set up here, in Cornwall, and I need to find it."

"And what makes you think I can help?" I stopped moving and looked him in the eye.

"We know you got a visit from one of them." He was calm and collected as he sat there with his hands linked on top of the table.

"You been spying on me?" I asked.

"We like to call it surveillance," he smirked.

"Did you see the Satan's go in and trash my house? While my family was there?" I shouted.

"We saw."

"You could have had them then. Breaking and entering. Why didn't you? They could have hurt one of my girls," I yelled, slamming my hand down on the table where he sat.

"We have our reasons. Now, are you going to help us?"

"Why would I help you?" I growled, taking a step back away from him. I kept chanting in my head 'Don't hit a police officer, don't hit a police officer, don't hit a police officer'.

"Because if you don't, you are going away for a very long time…" he paused, taking a sip of his coffee as we all stayed silent and waited for him to finish what he was saying.

"We've been tailing you for some time now, Blade. We've

seen what you get up to. Who you work for, the runs you do. We need your help to take down the Devon Destroyers MC."

"And what happens to me?" I asked through gritted teeth.

"You'll get a pass, slate wiped clean for helping us."

"FUCK!" I yelled. "And if I don't help?"

"Then you'll be coming with us right now, down to the station."

"Brett, what the hell man?" VP said to him. "You've been like one of us just without the patch. We've always helped each other out and now you go and do this?"

"It's my job. The Devon Destroyers are up to something and we need to get a handle on it."

"Do you know what will happen to him if they find out?" Solar asked him. Brett shrugged his shoulders. "They'll kill him, man."

"Then make sure they don't find out, simple."

"Simple?" I roared, throwing my hands up in the air.

"Are you in?" Brett asked, leaning forward so his elbows were on the table.

"Do I have to decide right this minute?" I asked.

"Yep and you have a month to figure it all out. I want the Devon Destroyers behind bars within one month."

"I need longer than that. Three months at least," I tried bargaining with him.

"I'll give you two."

"Fine," I agreed, against my better judgement. He held out his hand and I looked around at the other members, they subtly nodded and I shook his hand. Did I just make a deal with the devil? I needed to get out, I needed to ride. These guys knew me quite well now, especially Tat. I looked at him as he had Liam and he nodded his head, telling me to go. I knew Liam would be good with him and I knew they would all keep an eye on Heather, I wasn't running away, I needed to ride to form a plan and I needed to find a way to convince Heather to move back to Devon with me. I didn't want her at the clubhouse, I wanted her in our home.

Chapter 14

Heather

I was starting to get worried, Blade had been gone for hours. Tat had brought Liam back to me when he was getting fussy and all he told me was that Blade was on some 'Club business'. I hated that I didn't get to know any details. Kelsey was already fast asleep in bed and Liam and Tegan were being fussy. I had them both in my arms, one on each hip and their heads laid against my shoulders. I was pacing around the room trying to get them to sleep. Every time I stopped moving one would wake up and cry setting the other one off. This time they had woke Kelsey up too.

"Mummy," she said sleepily, rubbing her eyes.

"Sorry, sweetie. Do you want to sleep in with Ashlyn?" I asked her. She nodded, sucking her thumb and grabbing her teddy. "Come on then, can you open the door?" she nodded again. "Good girl." I found it difficult to do anything with two babies in my arms. "Knock on the door first," I said as she was about to walk into Ashlyn's room. We waited a few seconds before the door swung open.

"Hello," she smiled brightly, looking at us.

"I want to sleep wiv you." Kelsey said.

"Sweetie, you're meant to ask," I laughed.

"Oh, can I pwease sweep wiv you?" she asked.

"Of course." Ashlyn opened the door wider and Kelsey ran in and jumped on the bed.

"You sure you don't mind? These keep waking her up."

"Do you want some help?" She asked.

"No, they're just being fussy," I told her. "Thank you for

looking after her."

"I'm happy to have her, anytime." I smiled in thanks and walked back to my room, pacing again trying to lure the babies back to sleep.

They were nearly asleep when I heard the bedroom door open, I turned around to see Blade walking in. He looked tired, emotionally and physically.

"You ok?" I asked, walking towards him. I wanted to touch him but I couldn't, my hands were full. Liam let out an almighty cry which woke Tegan again. I sighed and bounced them both around.

"Here, give him to me." Blade said as he reached over to take Liam off me.

"He's been unsettled all day," I told him. As soon as Blade held him close he fell silent and I moved Tegan so she was laying in my arms, this was the position she liked to be in, but that was difficult when I had two babies to calm down. "You have the magic touch. He must have needed his daddy."

Blade gave me half a smile before putting Liam in his cot. Tegan was still awake and I wasn't going to risk putting her down and waking Liam back up.

"I need a shower." Blade grumbled, walking past me.

"Hey, you sure you're ok?" He shrugged his shoulders and walked away in silence.

Blade looked like he had something on his mind and I wanted to know what was bothering him, I knew that he wouldn't tell me but I had to at least give it a shot. As I put Tegan down next to Liam the bathroom door opened and Blade walked out with just a towel wrapped around his waist. He walked to his drawer and grabbed a pair of boxers.

"Wait, don't put them on yet." He glanced towards Kelsey's bed and raised his eyebrows. "She's with Ashlyn." He put the boxers back away and I locked the bedroom door. "Are you gonna tell me what's wrong?"

"I can't, you know that, sugar," he sighed, sitting on the edge of the bed. I climbed up behind him and began rubbing his shoulders.

"You're very tense. You need to relax…"

"I know a way you can relax me," he smiled.

"I already have a way planned," I whispered in his ear as I kissed him below it.

"Oh yeah?" He looked at me and I nodded.

"Lose the towel, lie on your front," he looked at me, eyebrows high on his head again. "I'm not telling you what to do, we're not having sex… Yet."

"Fine," he grumbled. He stood up and let the towel drop to the floor. He got comfy on the bed and I grabbed some fragranced oils. I straddled his hips and ran my oiled hands over his back, working the muscles in his back and shoulders. It was hard work on my hands as he was so big.

"How does that feel?" I asked, I didn't want to hurt him.

"Mmm, good. How come I've never had a massage from you before?" he asked. I shrugged my shoulders in answer. I carried on with his back and shoulders, I climbed off him and began working on his arms and hands. "I think you need to lose some clothing," he chuckled.

"I am a little bit hot," I said as I pretended to fan myself. I pulled my t-shirt and jeans off and stood in front of him in just my underwear. I grabbed more oil and began rubbing down his lower back, bum and legs. "How's that feel?"

"Good, it aches a little bit higher." I was rubbing his calf muscles, I moved up to his thighs.

"Here?" I asked.

"A little higher."

"Here?" I asked as I reached his bum.

"Yep, all around there," he smiled. I massaged his firm ass making sure it was well oiled when I noticed something.

"What's this?" I asked.

"What?" He leant up on his elbows and looked over his shoulder. "Oh, it's a tattoo,"

"And why do you have a 'T' tattooed on your ass?"

"It was a bet, we lost. Riz has a 'S' and CG has a 'U'," he chuckled again.

"That's a bit random."

"Yep, don't worry, it's not for an old girlfriend or anything."

"Good, now roll over so I can do your chest."

"Are you going to straddle me again?"

"Yes."

"Then I want you naked."

"Fine." I pulled my underwear off, grabbed the oil and climbed on top of him.

"I hope this isn't how you normally massage people," he smiled. That was a better look on his face then the worry I saw earlier.

"Kade!" I hissed. "No one else gets to see this body except for you." I leant forward and gave him a kiss, he wound his hand in my hair and deepened the kiss as he rose his hips and slipped inside of me. I gasped and Blade used the opportunity to slip his tongue into my mouth.

"I'm meant to be giving you a massage, not fucking you," I mumbled as he wouldn't let me go. After a couple seconds he released my hair and I went to climb off him, his hands clamped down on my hips as he thrust into my body.

"Aahh," I called out.

"Ssshh," he whispered, placing his hand over my mouth. "I can feel you pulsing around me. You want it as much as I do."

"Yes," I whispered throwing my head back as he played with my clit. "But this was meant to be for you, to relax you."

"I am very relaxed." I looked at him. "Ok, fine. Here," he poured some oil onto his chest and placed my hands in it. "Massage my chest as you ride me, sugar." I sat very still as I rubbed the oil into his chest. "Sugar, you're killing me," he groaned. I rotated my hips a couple of times. "You're torturing me," he complained. I was torturing him, I was slowly losing my will and I really wanted to bounce up and down on him. He had clearly had enough when he held me off the bed slightly and slammed into me a couple of times, I could see the muscles in his arms straining. I ran my hands over them and he lowered me back down. I leant forward, kissing him as he pounded into me. I could feel the familiar build up and I wanted to work it out of my body. I placed my hand on his chest, getting him to stop. I rose to my feet causing him to fall from my body and I turned around, I wanted him to see where he was entering my body, I wanted him to watch himself disappearing into me. I sat back down on him and he groaned. I wasted no time and began riding him hard and fast, I could feel myself trembling and I could feel him growing. I knew I wouldn't be able to keep quiet. "Kade," I panted. "I need to stop, I'm going to scream." Our movements halted as he sat up slightly and pulled me back on top of him, my back to his chest, we were still connected and he held me still as he pushed up into me a few more times, he placed his spare hand over my mouth to muffle the noises that were coming from me. As I came, I bit down onto his hand and he swore into my ear. We stayed connected for a few more minutes while we tried to breathe. I was feeling hot and sweaty and needed to move. I climbed off him as he protested.

"I need a shower," I told him.

"Not tonight. I want to hold you close like this, I love that you smell of me and sex. I love you, sugar."

"I love you too, baby." I snuggled against him and we fell asleep quickly after a vigorous workout.

Chapter 15

Blade

It had been several days since I made the agreement with the police, I still hadn't formed a plan in my head, I figured I'd need to head back there and see what was happening. I still had to approach the subject with Heather. There was no sign of any danger for weeks and Kelsey was getting bored being stuck in the clubhouse.

"Shall we go into town?" I asked Heather as she brushed Kelsey's long, brown, curly hair.

"Can we go to the park?" Kesley called out.

"Yes, sweetheart," I told her.

"Yay." She jumped up from the bed and grabbed her shoes. Liam and Tegan were in the middle of the bed kicking their legs and waving their arms. They were dressed for the day, Liam was in dark jeans and a t-shirt that said 'I'm a big brother' and Tegan was dressed in pink dungarees.

"Is it safe to go out?" Heather asked, standing in front of me.

"Yes. Besides, I'm not letting any of you out of my sight. You're all safe with me. I promise. I'll just let the guys know where we're going."

"Can you take them, so I can get ready?" She smiled up at me.

"Sure." I kissed her quickly on the lips. "Hurry up." I slapped her on the ass and she yelped in surprise and as she looked at me, I winked and blew her a kiss. She shook her head, laughing as she walked into the bathroom.

"Come on, Kelsey, let's go see the guys." She nodded and opened the door and ran ahead of me into the bar where the guys were probably eating after not getting out of bed before noon. I watched as she ran and jumped onto the sofa next to Solar, she grabbed the remote control out of his hand and turned the big screen TV onto cartoons. I chuckled as he sat there and watched with her while she was telling him all about it. Carla walked over and took Liam out of my arms, kissing him all over his face. When she pulled away and looked at him she was rewarded with a beaming smile.

"Mummy, can I hold him?" Olivia asked as she held out her arms.

"You have to sit on the sofa," she told her, Olivia nodded and ran over to the sofa. She sat holding her arms open and Carla placed Liam on her daughters lap, pushing a large cushion under his head to help Olivia support him. He wasn't small for a five month old that was born two weeks early. He was going to be a big boy.

"Drake?" I called out, he looked up at me and I nodded my head for him to come closer. Once he was getting closer I asked, "You get it?"

"Sure did, it's outside the door."

"Great. Thanks, man." I shook his hand and Heather looked at us as she walked towards me.

"What's all this?" she asked. I couldn't take my eyes off her, she was wearing a pair of light pink skinny jeans that could be classed as a second layer of skin, a strappy top and cardigan. She had on a pair of sandals that showed off her pink toenails and her hair was loose, flowing down her back.

"Nothing, you ready to go, sugar?" She kissed me gently and the taste of her strawberry lip gloss was my undoing and I pulled her closer, moving Tegan out of the way slightly. She whimpered against my lips and I had to step away before I left the kids with Carla and dragged her back to our room.

"Do you have a pushchair for Tegan? I've got one for Liam," she asked.

"No, it got trashed."

"Oh, what are we going to do then? We'll have to go and buy

a cheap one from somewhere."

"It's all sorted. Drake!" I called out and nodded my head and he walked outside, a few seconds later he came in. "There we go, sugar." She spun around to look behind her and she gasped as she walked closer to Drake who was pushing a twin pushchair.

"Is this ours?" she asked, smiling brightly as she ran her hands over the handle and across the red material.

"Yes, it's a travel system. The car seats click in there." I showed her where and she thanked me by stepping on her tip toes and winding her arms around my neck and showing the entire club who she belonged to.

"Come on, Kelsey, let's go!" Heather called out as she stepped away from me and Carla passed her Liam.

"Can uncle Solar come?" she asked, running towards us as Heather strapped the babies in their car seats.

"Does he want to come with us?" I chuckled.

"Yes. You do, don't you?" She looked around and asked him. He looked at me and I shrugged my shoulders at him. You could tell he wasn't really interested in coming out with us, but he didn't want to disappoint her either.

"Yes, I'd love to," he said with a bit too much enthusiasm. I rolled my eyes and we walked out to Heather's car; Kelsey had hold of Solar's hand. I secured Liam and Tegan in the car. There wasn't much room left in the back seat.

"Sugar, you'll have to sit in between the babies as Kelsey's car seat won't fit. She'll have to ride in the front." Heather nodded as she climbed in.

"I want to go with uncle Solar!" Kelsey called out.

"You can't sweetheart, he's riding his bike. But I bet if you ask him really nice, he'll go on the swings with you at the park." Her face lit up and she climbed into the car once I had her car seat in the front.

"We all ready?" I asked as I started the engine. Heather and Kelsey called out 'yes' and I laughed at how just leaving the clubhouse was like a military operation.

***

We had been out for a couple of hours, Kelsey had fun in the park and it was good that she had Solar running around after her instead of us. We had lunch in a small café as the babies and Kelsey needed feeding. We were now walking through the town, window shopping. I was in charge of the pushchair, Heather was walking with Kelsey who had one hand on the pushchair and one hand in Heathers.
"Where's uncle Solar?" Kelsey asked.
"He's just over the road," I began to say when I stopped in my tracks when I hear a startled scream.
"NATHAN!" I looked behind us and there was a frantic woman searching for something.
"Miss, are you ok?" I asked her.
"My son, he was here and now he's gone. I can't..." she paused as she looked up. "Nathan!" she screamed again. I followed the direction she was looking in and there was a small boy stood in the middle of the road, and a car was approaching. I went to run across the road when I spotted Solar who was closer to him.
"Solar!" I yelled, he looked at me and I nodded at the little boy. He didn't think, he ran and scooped the little boy out of the road just as a car sped around the corner blasting its horn. The little boy started crying and Solar rushed towards us, handing him off to his mother.
"Thank you, thank you, thank you so much," she kept repeating.
"Is he ok?" Heather asked.
"Yes, I think so." She began checking him over and he seemed fine.
"I'm Heather, this is Blade and Solar."
"Hi, I'm Jasmine and this is Nathan." She didn't look very old,

I would have said about twenty at most and her son looked about two.

"You need to keep a better eye on him." Solar grumbled at her.

"I do, it was only for a minute. This is the first time this has happened," she said in her defence as she clutched the boy close to her chest.

"Where's his dad?" Solar questioned. I had never seen him like this, he was angry and also concerned.

"Not that it's any of your business, but he died before Nathan was born."

"I'm sorry to hear that." Heather said.

"Well, I had best get him home. Thank you again... Is there any way I can repay you for your kindness?"

"Well..." Solar smirked. I slapped him on the back of the head and he glared at me.

"We're just glad he's safe," I told her. She nodded, smiled and began walking away. I watched as Solar kept his eyes on her until she disappeared. Once she was out of sight, he cleared his throat, snapped out of his daze and said goodbye as he made his way back to the clubhouse.

***

I walked into our bedroom after our short church meeting, I had informed the club that I was leaving tomorrow as I needed to get my plan into action. I needed to discover what the Destroyers were hiding and fast. Now was the difficult bit, telling Heather that I had to leave and hoping like hell that she would come with me.

I pushed the door open and the sight I saw stopped me in my tracks. Heather was wearing a t-shirt and her panties and she was leaning over the cot, so all I saw was her ass up high in the air. I whistled at her and she stood up quickly and looked over her shoulder.

"Shit, you scared me."

"Are they sleeping?" I asked, stalking towards her.

"Yeah, all flat out. I didn't even read a full page with Kelsey," she smiled, looking over her shoulder at her. She was fast asleep, thumb in her mouth and her teddy clutched to her chest.

"We need to talk."

"Oh… Why do I get the feeling I'm not going to like this?" I took her hands in mine and pulled her to our bed, we sat down facing each other.

"I have to go back to the Devon Destroyers MC."

"No, please, Kade. Don't leave us, not again," she sobbed. I tugged at her hands until she stood up and climbed into my lap, I maneuvered us so I had my back against the headboard. I ran my hand up and down her back.

"I'm not leaving you, we're all going." She sat up and looked at me.

"I can't go back to that clubhouse, Kade, you know I can't."

"Not to the club, to our home," I told her, looking at her in the eyes, trying to figure out how she felt about that. "Please, sugar. I have to go back but I don't want to be apart from you or the kids." She nodded her head and a sense of relief swamped my body. That was the first hurdle over with, now I just had to figure out the rest before I was locked up and away from Heather and our family for a long time.

Chapter 16

Heather

Blade and I had been up since the crack of dawn, he had gone into town to hire a van to get all of our stuff back to Devon and I was sad to be leaving Cornwall once again. The Cornish Crusaders were great to me and I wouldn't have got through everything without them. I had made some great friends and I hoped that I would still get to see them often. One of the most difficult things was going to be leaving Cammie, she was staying with Mason and I hated the thought of not seeing her every day. She was like a sister to me, I was a lot closer to her than I was with Daisy.

"I can't believe you're leaving." Cammie sobbed as we hugged each other.

"I know, I wish you were coming with us," I told her.

"I know, but my life is here now, with Mason." Cammie said. We broke apart and I wiped at the tears that were running down my face.

"Where's Daisy?" I asked looking around.

"She got up and left early this morning. She's been acting a bit strange recently." Carla added.

"I'll be back in a few days to check up on her, she's been a bit distant lately."

"Sugar, you ready?" Blade called out as he stood by the doors.

"Yes, where's Ashlyn?" I asked, walking closer to him.

"She's saying goodbye to the kids. They're strapped in the car, ready to go." Cammie took hold of my hand as we walked outside.

"Thank you for everything. All the help at the club and with

Liam and most importantly, thank you for keeping me together when Blade left. I'll never ever forget that. I love you."

"I love you too," she sobbed as we embraced one more time. When we pulled apart Mason was there to hold her, she had Mason wrapping his arms around her in an instant, and I gave him a kiss on the cheek as I said goodbye.

"Are you sure you're not coming with us?" I heard Blade ask Ashlyn as I got closer.

"No, the guys said I can stay here until I figure out what I want to do. It's time for you and your family. Be happy and I'll miss you all."

"You can visit anytime you want to," I told her as I pulled her close for a hug.

"Thank you. I will."

"Come on, sugar." Blade held my door open for me and I looked into the back seat.

"Where's Kelsey?"

"She wanted to ride with Solar in the van." I looked over and she was waving frantically like she was on a float in the carnival and she was just crowned carnival queen.

"Are you not riding your bike back?"

"No, Tat is riding it and then he'll come back with Solar in the van. That's two more to help us unload then."

"Ok, let's get going then, before I cry anymore." He kissed me on the lips and I smiled and waved as we drove away from the Cornish Crusaders and towards the Devon Destroyers.

***

"Why are we here?" Kelsey asked, holding onto my hand as we walked in through our home. I placed Tegan, who was fast asleep in her car seat, on the kitchen floor.

"This is our home now, sweetie." I crouched down in front of her and unzipped her jacket. She pulled her arms out and threw her coat on the floor before looking around. I picked her coat up and looked around to see Blade watching me. Liam was in his arms looking around.

"Don't pick up after her all the time, she'll need to learn to do stuff herself soon." I nodded in agreement, we probably did let her get away with so much at the minute, but we both knew that she needed rules and routine going forward. "I gotta help the guys unload our stuff," he told me as he passed Liam to me. I smiled and watched Liam get excited as I kissed him on his cheeks, blowing raspberries.

"Can we watch TV?" Kesley asked.

"What do you say?" I asked.

"Pwease?" She smiled. I nodded and sat on the sofa with her as she picked out a cartoon to watch. Liam was sitting up on my lap engrossed in the TV too. After a few minutes, Tegan began crying and I placed Liam in the corner of the sofa so he couldn't move. I went and pulled Tegan out of her car seat and brought her over to the sofa.

Chapter 17

Blade

I swung my leg over my bike as I got ready to take the small back roads and head for the Devon Destroyers clubhouse. I felt nervous and uncomfortable, if things went wrong with this plan then Heather could wind up being a single mum. She had already lost one husband, I hated to think what would happen if I was killed too. I shook my head as I zoomed down the road, that wasn't going to happen, I'd figure out a way to get what the police needed. I needed to gain their support and trust again. I never told them why I left, I just went. Prez was used to that though as I was an enforcer, I could go where I liked as long as I attended church meetings at least four times a year.

I pulled up to the large gate in front of the clubhouse, a prospect stepped out to greet me and I was pleased to see it was Wayne. I pulled my helmet off and offered him my hand to shake.

"Blade, man. Good to see you. You staying long?" Wayne asked as he shook my hand and opened the large gates for me.

"Long enough. How's things been?" I asked, nodding my head towards the building in front of us.

"Different lately."

"How so?"

"Prez has changed, man. He's drinking, fucking the girls and disappearing a lot more too. Gloria left him."

"Shit," I cursed. What have I got myself into? "Thanks, man." I looked at his leathers and noticed that he was still labelled a prospect. "They still haven't patched you in?"

"Na, in a couple of months I will have been a prospect for a year, so fingers crossed for then."

"Good luck, man. I'd be happy for you to be one of us."

"Thanks, Blade." I nodded at him before I rode away. Wayne always seemed genuine, he looked out for all of us and I was sure he would make a great brother.

I pulled up outside the clubhouse and parked my bike in line with the others that were already there. I climbed off and left my helmet hanging off the handlebars. Here goes nothing. I took a deep breath and waltzed into the clubhouse like I didn't have a care in the world. I took a moment to look around, Roxy was standing behind the bar; she looked bored, filing her nails and popping her chewing gum. Riz and Ripped were sitting on the sofa watching the TV. Bump had Chantelle straddling him and CG and Tiffany looked like they were having a heated discussion in the corner of the room. Her hands were flying around as she spoke and CG kept shaking his head at her. His eyes caught mine and he walked away from her and headed straight towards me.

"Blade! It's good to see you, man. I didn't think you'd come," he said as he slapped me on the back.

"This is still my club, you're all still my brothers. I wanted to make sure it wasn't falling apart," I laughed.

"Well, well, well, look who it is." I turned around once I heard the Prez. His greying beard was longer and bushier. His clothes were wrinkled, his hair was greasy and he looked tired.

"You ok, boss?" I asked, shaking his hand.

"Never better," he slurred. "You staying for the party?" I didn't really want to, I wanted to get home to Heather and the kids, but I had to show my support to the club and join in. I had to make sure Prez trusted me so he would let me in on whatever was going down.

"Yeah, wouldn't miss it," I smirked.

"Great, church bright and early tomorrow. You're sticking

around, right?" he asked.

"Yep," I nodded.

"Hi, Blade." Vicky purred as she walked up to me and placed her hand on my chest. I removed it and took a step back.

"The sweet buns missed you." Prez chuckled.

"I have an Old Lady, you know that," I said through gritted teeth.

"Oh yeah and how is sweet Heather, where is she? Not joining us?" He had a smirk on his face and I felt my temper rising. He was the reason that I was away from her, if he had been more careful and not gained the attention from the police, I wouldn't be here and in this situation. I had to push down my anger and play nice with him if I wanted him to trust me. I couldn't afford for him to be suspicious of why I had come back so quickly.

"Na, she's home…"

"A night away from the ball and chain… Who will you choose to fuck?" Ripped said from behind me, I didn't even hear him approach.

"Didn't you hear me? I have an Old Lady." I went to walk away when Prez grabbed my arm, halting my movements.

"I think a true brother would take the opportunity to have a bit of fun. We'll even give you free reign, have anyone you want." Prez said as he held his hand out showing all the women for me to choose from.

"Fine, I choose her." I said pointing at Tiffany. Her mouth dropped open and her blue eyes bulged from her face. She looked at CG and he stepped forward.

"She's not a sweet bun," he growled at me.

"She practically lives here and I don't see a property on her." Ripped chuckled. "I'd say she was fair game… Have fun, brother." He slapped me on the back and I looked at Tiffany again, she looked worried. Her eyes were red and it looked like she was about to cry.

"Come on." I grabbed her hand and began pulling her out of

the bar area.

"What the fuck are you doing, man?" CG shouted, stepping in front of me to stop me walking away.

"Having some fun," I smiled and winked at him. I had to put on a bloody good act to convince them they could trust me and that I was committed to the club.

"She's mine. I claimed her," he shouted in my face as Ripped and Riz grabbed him by both his arms holding him back.

"No properties, no claim." Ripped laughed.

"Come on, sweetheart," I smiled as I pulled Tiffany towards my room. I pushed the door open and we walked inside. She stood in the middle of the room looking nervous, twisting her hands together and looking at the floor. "I need a piss. Have a seat." I waved my hand directing it at the bed; that was the only place to sit in here. She looked like she was having an internal battle with herself, I wondered what she was thinking, was she trying to decide whether to stay or run? To disobey a club brother is a big no no in the MC world. It all depended on how smart this chick was.

I turned around and stalked into the bathroom, my heart banged against my chest when I saw Heather's toiletries lined up on the sink. I picked up her Lacoste pink perfume and sniffed it. My dick instantly grew and I quickly put the bottle down. I placed my hands on either side of the sink, and stared at my reflection in the mirror. I had a dilemma myself, did I stay and fuck this chick to get the trust I needed from the brothers? It would be a life or death situation, if she blabbed her mouth off saying we didn't fuck, they would grow suspicious. Could I trust her enough not to say anything? Would threatening her work? Or would she run off to CG and tell him what had happened. One thing for sure was that CG would never forgive me if I did fuck her and Heather, would she understand? Would I need to tell her? I could class this as club business and she would never need to know it had happened. I had to do what it took to survive, I had to look at the bigger picture. I needed them to trust me completely so I could take them down and spend the rest of my life with my family, with no need to keep looking over our shoulders, with no worrying that we were in danger.

I turned on the cold tap and splashed my face with water, I put my game face on and walked into the bedroom. I wasn't Kade, the man Heather loved and needed, I was Blade, Devon Destroyers member, bad ass biker who loved to fuck.

"Shit!" I cursed as soon as I saw a half-naked Tiffany spread out on my bed, the bed I shared and fucked Heather in. Shit. I needed to get her out of my head. I walked closer to her and sat on the edge of the bed at her hip. I placed one hand on the pillow by her head and whispered in her ear;

"Are you ready for me?" She shivered as my breath crawled over her skin.

"Are... Are you going to hurt me?" she quietly spoke.

"Sweetheart, I'm gonna make you feel things you've never felt before." I kissed the spot under her ear and she didn't flinch, she didn't shiver, she didn't moan. That was the spot Heather loved being kissed the most. Shit, I couldn't do it. I loved her too much to betray her. She was my life, my world and nothing the police or the MC did to me would make me lose her trust.

I pulled back and stood up by the bed, I ran my hands over my face and scratched at my beard that was forming; I really needed to shave. I needed to decide how I was going to play this, how was I going to stop her from telling CG that we didn't fuck. Could I trust him enough not to say anything to his dad? He was nothing like them so maybe I could trust him. I was snapped out of my thoughts when I felt a tugging on my jeans, I looked down to see Tiffany kneeling on the bed and she was pulling at my belt.

"What the fuck!" I snapped and stepped away just as I heard the door fly open and an angry CG standing there, a bottle of whiskey in one hand, half of its contents emptied.

"Don't you dare touch her," he slurred stumbling into the room. Tiffany jumped off the bed and ran over to him just as he was about to fall over. He grabbed hold of her hips and they both toppled to the floor, with her landing on top of him. I stood behind her to help them both up when the door was pushed open. I looked up and saw Prez and VP standing there, smirking.

"I didn't know there was a party going on in here," Ripped said stepping into the room.

"No party, just us three. She likes to be filled by two men." I tried to smile like I had hit the jackpot, but really all I wanted to do was leave.

"Maybe I'll stay, in case she can take another cock." Ripped said as he grabbed his junk through his jeans.

"Fuck off, man. Look at her, she's only tiny," I said.

"Michelle was only tiny but she liked triple penetration," he smirked.

"Get the hell out!" I shouted and he backed away, longing in his eyes to stay and join in. Once he left, I looked over my shoulder and saw that CG was passed out on the floor, Tiffany was still straddling him. "Get up," I told her and shoved her clothes back at her. "Get dressed."

"Aren't we going to…" she nodded towards the bed as she held her clothes to her chest.

"Do you want to?" She shook her head frantically causing her dark hair to cover her face. "Do you love him?"

"Yes," she whispered as she looked at CG passed out on the floor.

"Do you want to be his Old Lady?"

"I… I don't know. I don't know if I want to stay here."

"My Old Lady lives in our house, she's staying away from here; she doesn't like it either."

"Oh." She looked over to him again and I could see how she felt just from the look she was giving him, which worked well in my favour.

"Here's the thing, if anyone asks, we fucked." She gasped and her head snapped around to look at me, she shook her head. "If you tell anyone we didn't, I'll kill him. All you have to do is keep quiet."

"What about him? Can I tell him the truth?"

"No," she nodded and began pulling her clothes back on. "You had best stay here for a little while, make it believable."

"Where are you going?"

"Home." I walked towards the window and pushed it open, it was small but I would squeeze out of it. I needed Heather in my arms, I needed to smell her scent and feel her soft skin against mine. "I'm trusting you," I said. She nodded and I walked away quietly into the darkness.

***

I managed to roll my bike to the gates before starting it up, I didn't want anyone to see me disappearing. I made the quick journey home, I was desperate to get to Heather.

I unlocked the front door and walked inside, the house was dark and quiet. I didn't turn any lights on as I didn't want to wake anyone up. I crept quietly up the stairs and headed for our bedroom. We'd decided to try Liam and Tegan in a room together. Tegan was in the cot that I had brought for Lily, my unborn daughter and Liam was in his moses basket. We needed to get him a proper cot soon, before he grew out of that one. I checked on them and they were fast asleep. Kelsey had her own room across the hall from us, she was sound asleep too. I walked into our bedroom and climbed on the bed behind Heather. She moaned and turned around to face me.

"Hi," she smiled.

"Hi, sugar." I kissed her gently and pulled back when she murmured against my lips;

"What time is it?"

"Just gone midnight." She snuggled against my chest and

within seconds she was pulling away.

"Why do you smell like a club whore?"

I took a deep breath and decided to tell her what they wanted me to do at the club tonight, leaving out the part about me actually considering it. Technically, it wasn't club business so she could know. I wanted her to know in case it got back to her somehow. I knew how bitchy the sweet buns were and they would use anything to throw in her face.

"Oh my God, that's awful. Does having an Old Lady not mean anything to anyone anymore?" She climbed out of bed and was now pacing the room, she was wearing a pair of shorts and a tank top, her hair was all over the place and she looked sexy as hell. "Why did you go back, Kade?"

"You know that's club business, sugar."

"I am so fed up of hearing those words!" she yelled. "We're meant to be partners, a team. I should know everything that is going on."

"Well tough, I am not risking yours, or their lives by telling you club business. I will *not* go through that again."

"I'm a big girl, Kade, I can look after myself."

"Oh really," I said as I stalked towards her and pinned her arms to the side of her body and held her against the wall.

"Can you get out of this, sugar?" She struggled against me and I pushed her tighter into the wall. I placed my lips next to her ear. "They love it when you struggle, when you fight..."

"Stop it!" she cried out. "They've never come for me before." I released her and turned my back on her. "Kade, what is it?" she asked, placing her arms around my waist. I had to tell her, maybe it would make her stop going against me, stop asking for information. Make her more alert.

"They came for you," I quietly said. She unwound her arms from my waist and walked around to face me.

"What? When?" She was thinking and then it dawned on her. "Cammie?" I nodded. "They thought I was Cammie? That's why they took her?"

"Yes, so when I say its club business you don't ask any more questions, got it?" She nodded and looked at the floor, winding her arms around herself. Shit, I didn't want to scare her, I wanted her to be on guard, to be careful when I wasn't around. "Sugar?" She looked up at me. "I love you and can't lose you."

"I love you too. I'm sorry." She stretched up on her tiptoes and wound her arms around my neck. She nuzzled my neck and after a couple of minutes she pulled back. "You still smell like another woman and I don't like it." She pulled away and crossed her arms over her chest, pushing those breasts of hers up. My eyes zeroed in on them and my dick instantly grew hard. I moaned as I palmed myself trying to ease the throbbing. She watched every movement of my hand and when I looked up into her eyes, she was slightly flushed and her eyes were full of desire.

"I'm going for a shower. Grab the baby monitor and get your ass in there," I demanded. She wasted no time, she grabbed the monitor that would tell us if Liam or Tegan woke up, and followed me in. I left the bathroom door open slightly just in case Kelsey needed us and I started to worship the body of my beautiful woman.

Chapter 18

Blade

"Blade! Welcome back, brother." Prez said and all the guys joined in. I stumbled out of my room this morning, making it look like I was pleased with myself and acting like it was a bitch being up this early, when really I loved this time of day as it was when Tegan and Liam would wake up happy and active.

"Thanks, boss," I nodded at him. "So what's new?"

"Keen there a bit aren't you?" VP said as he crossed his arms over his chest.

"Got something to hide?" I chuckled.

"Nope," he smirked and I had a feeling that he was hiding something.

"Right, boys, we've got some business to attend to. Riz and Bump you two are on the daily checks of 'skins'."

"My pleasure, boss." Riz said, smiling. He was after the brunette that worked there, Beauty. She was slim with a slightly rounded ass and long dark hair. He had told us all before that she loved doggy style and he couldn't resist spanking her fine ass.

"Bump, there is a shipment that needs to be delivered."

"I'm on it, boss," he answered without any hesitation.

"CG find out all you can about the Cornish Crusaders, something is niggling at me and I can't figure out what. I want details on all brothers, prospects, Old Ladies, club whores and businesses."

"Sure," he agreed and he didn't waste any time in pulling out his laptop.

"Blade, go and spend some time with your family. We won't chuck you into anything too deep yet, relax and we'll call you if something comes up." I nodded my head but it kind of felt like he was trying to keep me away.

Knock. Knock.

"Yeah!" Prez yelled.

"Police are here." Dwayne panted as he pushed the door open and didn't look anywhere apart from at the Prez.

"Shit. Bump get that shipment out of here. Everyone, leave your weapons behind."

"You got it, boss." Prez slammed down the gavel and Bump ran out of the door and into the next room. We all removed our weapons before stepping out of the room.

"EVERYBODY FREEZE." I looked towards the door and four policemen were standing there, one of which was Brett. Was he checking up on me? If he blew my cover I was as good as dead. "HANDS WHERE I CAN SEE THEM." We all knew the protocol by now, we placed our hands on our heads including the club whores and Old Ladies that were around. No one dared to move, these guys meant business, and if they had a reason to shoot they would.

"What can we do for you gentlemen?" Prez asked.

"Just a friendly drop in call." Brett said as he walked further into the room.

"Then why are we standing like this then?" I asked. Brett looked at me surprised that I spoke to him that way.

"Let's do a pat down." Brett instructed the other officers.

"Hands on the wall." We all moved until we had our hands on the wall and legs spread. The officers began patting us down, I was at the end of the line and Brett had started with me.

"Anything yet?" he whispered. I subtly shook my head. "Times ticking."

"Get the fuck away or they'll suspect something," I growled.

"Clean!" Brett called out as he stepped away from me and I

walked towards the bar. I leant over and grabbed a bottle of beer, I needed it.

"All clear." One of the officers said.

"Keep out of trouble boys." Brett said as they walked away.

"What the fuck was that?" Prez yelled. "Get me a whiskey," he demanded and Roxy rushed around the bar and poured him a rather large shot. "Everyone watch your backs, they may be keeping an eye on us for some reason."

Everyone agreed and nodded their heads.

"Now get to work!" he shouted and everyone hurried away.

"Chantelle, come with me." The tall, leggy blonde didn't hesitate and she followed him out of the room. Roxy, Vicky, CG and me were the only ones left in the room and I sat in the chair opposite CG.

"Find anything out yet? What exactly is he looking for?"

"Yep and no idea," he said abruptly to me.

"What's crawled up your ass?"

"You," he started but paused to take a deep breath. "You slept with my woman when you have Heather and a family at home."

"No, no I didn't." I leaned back in my chair and took a swig of my beer.

"What?"

"I didn't sleep with her. I made it look like we did. You know how much I love Heather, I'd never do that to her. Besides, I only picked Tiffany as I knew she'd keep her mouth shut. Can't trust the other sweet buns."

"Ok, good." He carried on tapping away at his laptop and I kept quiet for a few minutes. I needed to find out if he knew anything about what his dad was up to.

"How's your dad been?" I casually asked.

"Drinking loads, fucking loads and…" I leant forward to hear what he was about to say.

"What you girls whispering about?" Ripped said as he sat next to CG.

"I was just telling him how sweet his girl tasted last night," I smirked as I finished my beer.

"Nice. I might have to get me some of that," he held his hand up for a high five and I slapped it as I stood up.

"It's official, she's my Old Lady. Got her leather and everything." CG pointed out.

"Ahh, so you don't mind used goods then for an Old Lady?" Ripped chuckled.

"Shut the fuck up." CG slammed his laptop closed and stormed away.

"Roxy, two more," he held his hand up and pointed towards me. "You staying for another, right?"

"Sure." This was my chance to get any info out of him. I had to think smart about this, all he loved to talk about was pussy. I sat back down. "The best thing I did was coming back here, hell, I got to pick any girl I wanted last night and let me tell you…" I stopped talking when Roxy walked over.

"Hi, Blade." She ran her hand over my head and I wanted to push her away but I knew I had to play the part.

"Hey, we're talking for a min, you know. Club business, I'll come find you in a minute." I winked at her and she giggled as she walked away, stopping to pick a bottle off the floor and showing me that she had no underwear on. There was her pussy, bare and pink staring at me.

"So, that Tiffany chick, any good?" He was eager for information and I didn't want to disappoint him but I didn't want to fuel any desires he had for her either. If CG said she was his Old Lady then Ripped wouldn't be able to touch her now. I went for it to gain his trust. I felt like we were two twelve year olds gossiping about our first kiss.

"Hell yeah, she's a wild cat. Likes it in every orifice."

"No way!" he shouted as he slammed his hand down on the table.

"She was like the energizer bunny, I had trouble keeping up. Best ride of my life," I told him, picturing Heather riding me when she was pregnant with Liam and coming all over my cock. That was the best ride of my life. Shit, I was getting hard, not the best moment for that.

"You going there in a minute?" he asked, nodding towards Roxy who was wiping down the bar watching us, she was waiting for me to call her over so I could fuck her.

"Yeah, man, unless you want her?" I offered.

"Na, she's ok. I want some new pussy. We need some new whores around here. Especially now there's no Cammie."

"Had a soft spot for her did ya?" I asked as I tipped my head back and downed my drink.

"She'd let me do anything to her and I mean anything." I hated hearing him talk about Cammie that way, she was like a sister to me and it made me protective of her, but I couldn't let it show. "So what about your Old Lady? Not giving it to you anymore?"

"Here and there..."

"I bet that baby ruined her pussy, I can't imagine fucking a woman who's had a child."

"You fucked Cammie," I stated.

"She's not a mum," he chuckled.

"She had a baby, he was still born," I informed him, peeling at the label on the beer bottle.

"Shit. You could never tell, brilliant I can add chicks who have had kids back onto my fuck list," he smiled like he was proud of himself.

"I'm bored, I don't wanna go home to a house full of screaming kids. You got anything on?"

"Well..." he started saying when the Prez interrupted us.

"VP, let's go."

"Sorry, man. I'll leave you to have some fun of your own." He meant Roxy and I couldn't think of anything worse.

"Thanks, man. Catch ya later." I walked away from him and up to the bar, I tried to listen to what the Prez was saying to him but couldn't hear from Roxy talking my ear off. This bitch was annoying the crap out of me.

"So?" she asked.

"Huh? What?" I couldn't recall a single thing she had said.

"Where to and how do you want me?" She started undoing the buttons on her shirt and I took a step back.

"Sorry, I gotta get back to my Old Lady." I winked at her and walked away, I was hoping to see where the Prez and Ripped went but I couldn't make it obvious and follow them out.

I got to my bike and noticed that all the other bikes were gone, which meant I missed out on an opportunity to follow them.

"FUCK!" I shouted and slammed my fist into the wooden fence that was beside me.

***

I pulled up to my house and was surprised to see a bike sitting in the driveway. I couldn't think whose bike it was, I panicked that they were all in danger and rushed into the house.

"Sugar?" I called out.

"In here," she called back, I followed her voice and she was in the living room, Liam and Tegan were laying on an activity mat and Kelsey was laying on her front colouring in. I looked into the eyes of a man I hadn't seen for over ten years.

"What the fuck are you doing here?" I shouted.

"Daddy, you said a bad word." Kelsey sung, not looking up from her colouring book.

"Kade!" Heather hissed at me. I was clenching and unclenching my fists and could feel the pain in my right hand where I had punched the fence, but it wouldn't stop me punching this guy in the face. I didn't want him here, around my woman and kids.

"Now, is that anyway to greet your father? I wanted to come and see my grandchildren."

"Kitchen, now!" I growled at him. I turned around and walked away from him. I heard him following me, what was he doing here?

"Now, Kade, listen before…"

"Blade," I told him, cutting him off.

"Sorry, Blade…"

"Did you even visit her?" I asked, cutting him off again. He looked confused. "Kayleigh, did you see her before she died?"

"I wanted to…"

"She was your fucking daughter and you couldn't spare a day to go and see her. She almost died alone!" I shouted.

"Kade?" Heather whispered behind me and I held out my hand for her, not looking at her. She grabbed it and we stood together as a united front.

"It's ok, sugar, he was just leaving." I stared at my dad and waited for him to argue.

"K… Blade, I need your help."

"Not now," I growled at him, he had been an enforcer just like me for an MC in Somerset. He knew the rules, no talking about it in front of Old Ladies. I started walking him to the door, Heather hot on my heels.

"They're gonna kill me," he said as he stepped outside. I heard Heather gasp and I looked at her to see her hand covering her mouth. I looked at the man standing in front of me, he was fifty seven, had grey strands covering his head and beard, his jeans were old and had holes in them, his leather jacket was worn, a Somerset Saints & Sinners patch covering it.

"I don't wanna hear it," I told him.

"Kade!" Heather snapped at me.

"Get in the house!" Her mouth opened to speak and I shouted, "NOW!" She hurried off, shutting the door behind her and I stalked towards my dad, pushing his strong body up against the fence.

"You *do not* come in here and talk in front of my Old Lady. I *will not* have her involved. I have a family to protect." I stepped away from him and ran my hands over my face, I didn't need this now. I had so much on my plate I didn't need to fight his battles for him too.

"It wasn't my fault you know, her death."

"It was cancer," I stated. Did he not even know how his own daughter died? He was never there for us when we were growing up, if I got into fights at school he never tried to help, he always said, 'Fight back, what are you a pussy'.

"Not Kayleigh, your mother."

"Not your fault!" I screamed at him, my face close to his. "A bomb was put in her car! A rival club sent you a message and used her to do it. How is that not your fault?"

"I..."

"Get the fuck away, you deserve what's coming to you. As far as I'm concerned, they are my only family left," I yelled, pointing at the house behind me.

"I can help you, I can get the information you need."

"What? How did you..."

"I have contacts in the police force, when I heard your name mentioned I needed to know what they had on you."

"Can you make the threat the police have over me go away?"

"I'm afraid not, son. But I have information on the Destroyers warehouse in Cornwall. They..."

"Not here." I was always unsure of who could be around and listening. "I'll meet you later, at the beach. Midnight." He nodded in agreement, he straddled his bike and rode away from me. Was he finally going to be the dad I needed? Finally be someone I could trust to help me?

"Daddy?" a little voice chirped behind me. I spun around to see Kelsey looking at me as she held out a piece of paper for me.

"What's that, sweetheart?" I asked, picking her up and looking at the drawing.

"That's you, mummy, Teg and Li. That's me, in pink." She smiled, proud of her drawing.

"That's really great. Have you shown mummy?" she nodded,

kissed me on the cheek and wriggled to get down. She ran off back into the living room and I followed behind her quietly, stretching my hand out, it still hurt from where I had hit the fence earlier. I needed some ice on it. I walked into the kitchen and pulled open the freezer looking for ice cubes.

"What you doing?" Heather asked.

"Looking for some ice." I held up my hand to show her.

"Shit, Kade. Did you hit him?" She didn't sound pleased, I couldn't find any ice so I shut the door and turned around to face her.

"No, I hit a fence at the clubhouse earlier." She rolled her eyes and grabbed my hand to look at it.

"You've got splinters in the cuts. Sit down." She pointed to a stool at the breakfast bar as she began digging around in a cupboard.

"What are you doing?" I asked as she came closer.

"Getting the splinters out and patching you up," she smiled, showing me the first aid kit. My heart slammed against my chest, she wanted to take care of me. I loved that. I sat still while she pulled out little splinters of wood and cleaned out the wound and then wrapped my hand in a bandage.

"I love you, sugar," I smiled at her, pulling her close to me and claiming her lips.

"And so you should," she giggled, pulling away from me.

"Where are you going?" I wanted more than just a kiss and she knew it. She nodded her head behind me and I looked over my shoulder to see Kelsey watching us. "You ok, sweetheart?" I asked her.

"Why are you always kissing mummy?" she asked, tilting her head, making her dark curls bounce around. She walked towards me and I picked her up and sat her on my lap.

"Because I love her," I smiled, looking over the top of her head at Heather.

"Do you love me?"

"Of course I do." I pecked kisses all over her face, I loved hearing the sounds of her giggling.

Chapter 19

Blade

I was lying in bed, wide awake, watching the sun start to filter through the cracks in the curtains. It was going to be a bright and sunny day. It was a shame that my mood wasn't going to match it. My head had been non-stop all night, trying to digest all that my dad had told me.

I would check in with the club, but if they didn't need me I was going to head to Cornwall and check out this warehouse and see what it was being used for. I needed some information to feed back to the police so they knew I was taking this seriously.

"Morning," I heard Heather moan beside me. I looked over and saw her stretching, she thrust her tits up in the air and within seconds I was on top of her, sucking a nipple into my mouth through the thin material of her top. "Mmm," she moaned, holding my head closer.

My body was on edge, and I needed to feel all of her to calm myself down. I released her nipple and slammed my mouth down onto hers, she wound her hands around the back of my neck, kissing me back with just as much force. I nudged her legs apart with my knees and started rubbing my hard cock over her pussy, I could feel how warm and wet she was through her tiny bed shorts.

"Kade," she moaned as she arched her back. "I need to feel you."

"Oh, sugar. You're going to feel me, don't you worry," I chuckled, barely pulling away from her delectable mouth. Her lips were soft and always tasted like strawberries. Anytime I smelt the scent, it always had me picturing her lips and kisses. We always wore clothes to bed now, which I hated. But we didn't want to run the risk of Kelsey walking in and seeing us naked. I was glad that it had only just hit six in the morning and Kelsey and the babies wouldn't start waking up for at least an hour yet.

I pulled back from her and began stripping her of her clothes, kissing her skin as soon as it became visible. Her body was curvy and toned, she had a few small stretch marks on her tummy, but that only made her sexier to me. I ran my lips over her tummy and mound as I pulled her shorts down slowly. I looked up to see her eyes trained on me, they were closed slightly and she tried rubbing her thighs together but I held them apart as I kissed the insides of her thighs and down her legs, making sure I didn't miss a spot.

"Kade, please?" she panted. I could never resist her when she begged, saying my name. I settled myself in between her legs, pushed them open as far as they would go and attacked her with my mouth. At the first taste, I was hooked. I explored every part of her, bringing her to orgasm twice. She had coated my chin in her release and her legs were clenched firmly around my head. I had to tap her on the leg to get her to release me. I stripped out of my boxers and kissed my way up her body. Once I was looking into her eyes, she grabbed my head and devoured my mouth, moaning as she could taste her arousal on my tongue. As we kissed, I lined myself up to her entrance and moved in slowly. She arched her back which caused our lips to break apart, and I concentrated on not blowing my load in two seconds flat. Once I was stretching her, I couldn't hold back and I reared back and slammed back into her causing her to shift up the bed.

"Hold on, sugar," I smirked as I kissed her again. She wound her arms and legs around me and held on as I set a punishing rhythm of slamming in and out of her small body. I knew when she was close to release when her grip with her thighs got stronger and he nails dug into my back. Once her body softened, she unwrapped herself from around me and I kissed her gently, pulling her nipples in between my thumb and finger. I moved in and out of her slowly, trailing kisses over her neck, making sure I hit that spot behind her ear that she loved so much, her body quivered and she arched into me, telling me that she was ready again. After this session, she would be feeling me all day and I loved that thought.

I pulled her legs so that her thighs were flat against my chest, and I pushed forward so they were almost touching her chest. I loved how flexible she was, the yoga definitely helped with that. She moaned and fisted the sheets underneath us in her hands. Her eyes were closed, her lips were parted and her skin was growing flushed. I pushed in and out of her in short quick thrusts.

"Kade," she panted. Opening her eyes, she locked gazes with me and whispered, "More." I pulled out of her and she whimpered at the loss of our connection, my girl was greedy this morning. I pushed my fingers inside of her and spread her juices down her body, running them over her other hole. She watched me and as I went to push my finger inside she tensed.

"Have you ever?" She shook her head, biting her lip. "It'll feel good, I promise. Relax for me, sugar." I sucked one of her nipples into my mouth and I heard her moan. Knowing she was distracted, I pushed my finger in up to my knuckle. I could feel her pulsing around me. I withdrew slowly, "On your knees, Sugar." She flipped herself over and climbed onto her hands and knees. I pushed my cock back into her greedy pussy, her head dipped as she moaned. Once my rhythm was steady, I parted her ass cheeks and slipped my finger back into her. She gasped and I stopped moving, I didn't want to hurt her.

"Kade, I..." she panted, pushing back into me. I started a punishing rhythm and she collapsed onto her forearms.

"Let go, sugar." She nodded and her hands gripped onto the pillow in front of her, she screamed out in pleasure and tightened around my cock and finger. Once she started pulsing I slammed in a few more times, groaning when I released into her warmth. I lay my forehead onto her back, I could feel the sweat between our bodies and our breathing was uneven. Once we calmed down, I pulled out of her and kissed her once more.

"Daddy, is it time to get up?" I heard Kelsey calling from the hallway. I jumped off the bed, threw Heather over my shoulder and raced into the bathroom. I didn't want her to catch us like that, it'd scar her for life. I remembered the few times I walked in on my mum and dad and that wasn't pretty. My semi hard cock had softened immediately and I willed the images to leave my head, shuddering I turned towards the shower and hit the on button, the hot water came pouring out and the bathroom was soon steaming up.

"Mummy? Daddy?" Kelsey called out.

"You get in and I'll see if she's ok," I told Heather as I kissed her quickly. I wrapped a towel around my waist and walked out into the bedroom. "You ok, sweetheart?" I asked as I looked at Kelsey who was laying in the middle of our bed, I dreaded to think what she was lying on. I scooped her up and kissed her nose.

"I thought I heard a scream, it woke me up," she pouted.

"Do you want to go back to sleep?" I started heading towards the door and to her room when she shook her head.

"I'm hungry."

"Ok, can you be very quiet and sneak into the babies' room and see if they are still sleeping?"

"Yes," she whispered, holding her finger over her lips. She quietly tiptoed towards their room and I dashed back into our bedroom to grab my jeans and a t shirt. I quickly pulled the towel away and slipped into my jeans.

"No boxers, huh?" I chuckled as I heard Heather talk. I turned around to see her leaning on the door frame, a towel wrapped around her body and her wet hair around her shoulders. I had images of wrapping that wet hair around my fist, pushing her over the arm of the small sofa we had at the bottom of our bed and fucking her from behind as I felt her legs quiver with trying to hold herself up. I went to take a step towards her when she smiled and pointed behind me. I looked over my shoulder and Kelsey was standing there.

"They still sleeping, Daddy," she whispered. I chuckled, turned around, picked her up and we both blew Heather a kiss before we went downstairs to make breakfast.

Chapter 20

Blade

After I had a lovely morning with my family, I stopped by the club. Prez and VP were nowhere to be seen, again. The other guys didn't seem bothered at their disappearing act but something felt unsettled about it. After I had hung around the club for a few hours, I was getting restless and needed to do something productive, so here I was riding on the small Cornish roads to the address my dad had given me. I was lost in thoughts when a bike pulled up beside me, I looked over and noticed it was a Somerset S&S patch. I shook my head at the thought that my dad was here, I hadn't seen him so much for years. I stopped at the first layby I came to and removed my helmet, knowing that my dad would follow me in.

"What you doing here, old man?" I asked, not bothering to get off my bike.

"You can't go in there alone, are you crazy?" He scolded me like I was eight years old again and was caught playing with matches.

"I'm just checking the place out, I want to see what the Prez is up to." I shrugged my shoulders like it was no big deal.

"And what if he's there? You gonna confront him? With no back up?"

"Hell no, I'm not stupid... Let's just head there and see." I pushed my helmet onto my head and started my bike up.

"Son, there is a wooded area just up from the warehouse, a good place to stash the bikes." I nodded my understanding and took off. I knew I was stupid coming alone, but I was only planning on seeing where this place was and if anyone else was involved, if this was a club venture then I wanted to know why I was being kept out of it.

I saw the place my dad mentioned and pulled up behind a line of trees. I got off my bike and placed my helmet on the handle bars. There was a warehouse sitting alone, several cars were surrounding the building. There was two guys standing outside the main door, I couldn't make out what cuts they had on. They didn't look like anyone in the Devon Destroyers that I knew. How were we going to get closer without being seen? All I wanted to do was look in through one of the windows and see what was being guarded.

"I'll create a diversion." Dad said. He knew exactly what I was thinking.

"No…"

"It's the only way you'll get to see inside." He was right, I knew he was. I nodded in agreement and hoped that he wasn't about to get himself killed. Why was he helping me? So I would help him back in return? I was lost in my own thoughts when I heard a bike rev, I looked up and saw that it was my dad and he had started riding towards the warehouse. As he got closer I saw the two guys on guard straighten up and pull out their guns. Shit. I had to get moving and quick. I walked through the woods until I was in line with one of the windows that was just around the corner #from where the guards stood. I could hear my dad talking to them, saying something about being lost. I tried to keep as low as I could, stopping behind anything that would hide me. I was standing behind a van when I heard some shouting going on inside, I looked at my dad and he gestured for me to get closer. I took a gamble and ran for the window. I peeked inside and saw loads of women surrounding the outside of the room. A Devon Destroyers jacket was facing me and I recognised that as Ripped. When he took a step to the side, I saw Prez and Gloria. Prez had his wife tied to a chair and she was gagged, she looked tired and beaten up. I ducked low as

Ripped turned around, shit that was close. I heard the roar of an engine and knew that was my warning to get out of there, my dad's diversion was ending and I needed to get back to safety.

***

Dad followed me all the way home and once we had stopped in my driveway he began getting off his bike.

"Don't you have a club to get back to?" I asked.

"I'd rather help protect my son," he told me.

"Well, that's a first." I heard the front door open.

"Kade, Ray. Why don't you both come on in? Food's almost ready." Heather said.

"Sugar, he's gotta get back," I told her as I walked closer and pulled her close against my body.

"Don't be silly, you can eat first, right?"

"That would be lovely. Thank you, Heather." Dad said as he walked past me and into my home.

"Sugar…"

"No, don't. He's family." She slid her hand down my arm until her hand was in mine and she pulled me into the house. As soon as the front door was shut I had her pinned up against it, I crowded her personal space and I heard her breath hitch in her throat. I lowered my lips closer to hers and her tongue darted out to wet them. Her eyes closed in anticipation of my kiss and I moved directions and went to her ear.

"Sugar, don't invite that man here again without asking me first or I'll have to make that ass of yours red."

"That's not really a threat, Kade," she giggled.

"Grandpa, where's mummy and daddy?" I heard Kelsey asking.

"They are having a talk in the hall. Let's leave them to it for a moment. What's that?"

"My colouring book. I'll show you."

"Grandpa?" I asked, eyebrows raised.

"That's what he is," she smiled.

He had distracted our daughter so I could get some alone time with Heather, I guess he couldn't have been that bad after all.

***

Heather

It was nice having Blade and his dad sitting at the dinner table. I had made a simple tea of fish pie, it was quite difficult trying to keep three children entertained throughout the day.

"Here we go," I said as I placed Blade and Ray's food in front of them.

"Sweetheart, this looks lovely. Been a long time since I've had a home cooked meal." Ray smiled at me.

"You're very welcome, anytime." Blade's head snapped towards me and I smiled knowingly at him and his threat he made earlier. I smiled back, trailing my hand up his arm as I walked back into the kitchen. I brought over mine and Kelsey's plates. The babies had already been fed and they were in their bouncy seats where we could keep a close eye on them. I was about to start eating when my phone started ringing. I looked over to where it was laying on the kitchen side, as I went to get up Blade said;

"Leave it and enjoy your food."

"It may be important." I grabbed it off the side and looked at the caller display. "It's Cammie," I smiled. "Sorry, you carry on."

I walked into the living room and answered the phone.

"Hey, you ok?" I listened to Cammie talking for a few minutes. "Oh, ok. I'll come up tomorrow… Yeah, I'll have them all with me. Can't wait to see you. Love you." I hung up the phone and walked back into the kitchen. I wasn't paying attention as my thoughts were on the conversation that Cammie and I just had.

"You ok, sugar?" I felt Blade's hand on mine as I sat down.

"I have to go to Cornwall tomorrow," I told him as I picked my fork up and began to eat.

"Wanna tell me why?" he asked.

"Oh, sorry. Cammie said that Daisy is acting strange, she keeps disappearing a lot and she is worried about her. I need to see what's going on."

"I'll come with you."

"Really? You don't have to be at the club?"

"They can cope without me for one day," he shrugged his shoulders like it was no big deal, but to me it was. "She's your sister, she's family."

I leant over the table and gave him a quick kiss.

"They always do that, Grandpa." Kelsey complained.

"Do they?" he asked.

"Yep, daddy said it's cuz he loves mummy." She placed her fork on her plate and pushed it away from herself. "Finished, can I av ice cream now?"

"Kelsey, you've hardly eaten anything," I said to her.

"I don't want it. I want some ice cream."

"You eat two more big mouthfuls and we'll see about that ice cream." Blade told her.

"Do it like grandpa," I told her as Ray shovelled his food into his mouth. Maybe not a great idea.

After we finished eating Ray and Blade went outside to talk while I got the babies ready for a bath and bed.

Chapter 21

Heather

I was just climbing into bed when I heard the front door close. The sound of heavy footsteps coming up the stairs had my body on fire. My sexy man didn't even need to be in the room to make me hot and needy.

I had bathed all the kids and got them to bed, Kelsey was a bit restless but I knew she would soon fall asleep.

The bedroom door opened and Blade stood filling the entire space, his arms were crossed over his wide chest and my eyes wandered over his sculptured body.

"Like what you see, sugar?" he smirked. I nodded and he casually walked through the door way closing it securely behind him. His eyes were dark and I could see the need for me in them. Once he was standing beside the bed, he pulled the covers off me and his eyes travelled over my bare white legs, I went to bed wearing a large t-shirt of his. He grabbed my hand and pulled me out of bed so I was standing in front of him. He took another step closer so that our bodies were touching and I had to lean back to look up at him. He lowered his head to my ear.

"Someone was being naughty earlier," he whispered in a low, sexy voice. Oh I loved it when he whispered, it sent shivers all over my body and I trembled in anticipation. I reached out to touch him and he pinned my arms to the side of my body.

"Did you deliberately do what I asked you not to, so you could feel my hand on your ass?" I pulled my bottom lip in between my teeth and shook my head, looking up at him through my eyelashes. "I think someone is lying..." He grabbed the bottom of the t-shirt and pulled it off over my head. My hair bounced and fell around my shoulders, covering the tips of my nipples. "No underwear?" His eyebrows rose and he looked pleased.

"There was no point, you'd only rip them off anyway," I smiled. He took a step back, leaving me standing there naked while he was still fully clothed. He sat down on the edge of the bed and before I knew what was happening he pulled on my wrist and my body was laying across his lap, bum high in the air. I tried to sit up and he placed his large rough hand on my back keeping me in positon. I squeezed my legs together trying to calm the throbbing sensation working its way through my clit, Blade obviously knew what I was doing as he parted my legs slightly.

"Now, sugar, do you know what you did wrong?" I shook my head and his hand came down and slapped my bare thigh. I gasped and squirmed in his lap, I could feel him hardening underneath me and that made the pulsing around my body worse. "Let's try again… Should you have invited my dad over to eat with us?"

"Yes, he's family," I whispered. Slap. This time it was on my bum cheek and I cried out in pain and pleasure, the slap stung but it also did wonderful things to my body. I was breathless, hot and needed him to release some of the pressure surrounding my clit. I felt like I was going to explode if he didn't touch me soon. "Kade," I pleaded.

"Wrong answer." His hand came down twice in a row, slapping different areas on my bum. I cried out as the frustration of not being able to climax was getting to me. "Please, Kade," I begged.

"Will you do it again?" His hand was still pressed firmly in the middle of my back keeping me still while his other one roamed up and down my legs, I found it difficult to concentrate. "Sugar?" he growled as another slap hit my leg. "No, no, I won't," I panted.

"Good girl." His hand moved and I cried out as he slipped two fingers inside of me. "You're very wet. I think my girl likes to be spanked." He stilled his fingers and I begged him to move them, trying to move my body to gain some friction. He pulled out of me and licked his fingers clean. Just as I was about to complain some more, he quickly moved our positons. I was now face down over the edge of the bed, my cheek against the softness of the sheets. I heard him pulling at his jeans and before I knew it he was filling me. He was still fully clothed and I could feel the light material of his t-shirt on my back.

"Yes!" I called out as I tried to lean up on my hands so I could push back against him, to feel him deeper and harder. Blade pushed me back down and kept his hand there while he slammed in and out of me, I couldn't move. My body burned, my spine tingled and I knew I was close to coming.

"Come on, sugar. Let go," he demanded, not slowing his pace down. He relentlessly pumped himself in and out of my body. My orgasm hit as he slapped me on the bum one last time, my walls tightened and he groaned as he emptied himself into me.

"Shit, sugar. Kelsey." Blade moved off my body and as I looked over towards the door I saw the handle moving. I shot up off the bed and grabbed my t-shirt that was laying on the floor, Blade was tucking himself in just as the door pushed open and he stood in front of me blocking me as I quickly pulled the t-shirt over my head and climbed into bed. "What are you doing out of bed?" Blade moved closer towards her and she held her arms out for him to pick her up.

"I had a bad dream," she sobbed. "There are monsters under my bed." She wrapped her arms around his neck and he kissed her on the top of her head.

"There are no monsters under your bed, shall I show you?" She shook her head frantically and it looked like her grip tightened on his neck.

"Kade?" He turned around to look at me and I patted the empty bed beside me. He walked over and placed her beside me. She curled into my side and I stroked her hair, trying to get her to go back to sleep.

"I'm going for a shower." He kissed me briefly before he walked into the en-suite.

Blade

I quickly stripped out of my clothes and turned the shower to hot. I hadn't had a moment to myself to think of everything that I had seen, I needed time to process it all.

When we found that sex trafficking place with the Cornish Crusaders, I saw two bikes pulling away in Devon Destroyers cuts. Was that Prez and VP?

Why did the Prez have his Old Lady tied up to a chair?

What were Prez and VP up to?

I had some digging I needed to do, the police would be hounding me for information soon and I wasn't going to risk my family's safety by being locked in a prison cell where I couldn't protect them.

I quickly scrubbed at my body, hating that I was cleaning Heather's scent off me. I needed her close, she was the only person in this world that could calm the rage and frustration building inside me. I turned the shower off, grabbed a towel and quickly dried off. I slipped into a pair of boxers, brushed my teeth quickly and strolled into the bedroom. Heather and Kelsey were both fast asleep. I leant over Heather and picked Kelsey up, I didn't want to disturb her but I needed my woman close to me tonight. I carried Kelsey back to her room and tucked her into her bed, she didn't wake up; I kissed the top of her head and quietly made my way back to bed. I climbed in beside Heather and she automatically turned her body so she was cuddled up against my chest. I looked down at her and she was still sleeping soundly. I traced my fingers up and down her back, it was relaxing and calming for me. I tried to empty my mind of everything and enjoy this moment with her.

Chapter 22

Blade

"Sugar, I'm just gonna head to the club. Did you want to meet me there?" I asked as she changed Liam's nappy. Tegan was laying on the floor kicking her legs in the air and Kelsey was watching TV.
"You don't have to come with me if you're busy."
"Meet me in an hour. I'm coming with you." I turned her face towards mine and gave her a lingering kiss. When I began pulling back, she gripped the back of my head and deepened it. "Shit, sugar, I can't ride with a stiff one in my jeans." She giggled as she picked Liam up and placed him on her hip.
"Love you," she smiled.
"Love you too, see you in an hour." I kissed her quickly before walking out the door and heading to the club.

***

"I was just about to call you." CG said as I walked in through the clubhouse doors.
"Oh yeah?" I stopped in front of him, waiting for him to tell me why.
"Church meeting." I nodded in understanding and followed him through the door. Everyone was already in there sitting down and there was an awkward silence. I looked over to the Prez and he had his gun laying on the table in front of him, his hands were balled into fists like he was stopping himself from grabbing the gun and shooting.
"Boss," I nodded my head at him in greeting.

"Just sit the fuck down!" His jaw was clenched tight and I wondered what the hell was going on. Was I the only one who was clueless? Was this to do with me? Had they found out that I am working with the police? I tried to act as calm as possible, I couldn't let my body language give me away.

"First order of business," Prez began and his eyes locked on mine. "Blade…" he paused and my heart beat frantically. Was this it? Was I not going to see my family again? Not get to kiss Heather again? Or hold Kelsey, Tegan and Liam again? "It's good to have you back, we're having a party. Leave the Old Lady at home and come and enjoy the pussy." I breathed a sigh of release.

"Sure thing, boss."

"Next, VP and Riz got pulled over by the police yesterday. They were followed for miles so it wasn't just a coincidence. They were looking for something, luckily they had already done the drop else they would currently be sitting in a prison cell." He flexed his hands open and closed on the top of the table where we all could see. "My question is, how did they know about it?" Everyone, including myself, stayed quiet. I didn't even know about a drug run. "If we've got a rat at this table, I will soon discover who it is and then…" He grabbed his gun and shot a hole in the wall at the back of the room. The guys sitting at that end of the table all fell to the floor, protecting themselves. "Now get the hell out!" He slammed the gavel down and we all hurried out of the room. A rat at the table? I didn't even know about the drug run, which meant there was potentially someone else working against the club too. If I could figure out who it was we could join forces and take them down quicker. I didn't even know where to start.

"Yo, Blade." My thoughts were interrupted, I looked up to see Wayne staring at me. "Your Old Lady is outside. She said she won't come in."

"Tell her I'll be two minutes." He nodded and disappeared

outside again. I walked quickly to the bar where CG was sitting, tapping away on his laptop. I stood beside him leaning on the bar. "A rat? Can you believe that?"

"I know, shocked the hell outta me too." He didn't look up from his laptop as we talked.

"Do these guys not know what happens to a rat?"

"I guess not," he shrugged. He wasn't giving anything away and I would be really surprised if he went up against his dad. I looked around the room at the other guys and I couldn't even begin to imagine any of these would be a rat either, but then I guess they may think the same about me.

Heather

I was standing outside my car waiting for Blade and talking to Wayne.

"Heather?" I looked around and Tiffany was smiling at me.

"Hi, how are you?" I asked as I walked towards her and gave her a hug. "Still here, huh?"

"Yeah, I'm good. How's Liam?"

"Great, we have some new additions now too." I nodded my head towards the car, telling her to follow me. I opened the back door and she poked her head in.

"Who are these?" she asked, looking at Tegan in the back and Kelsey who was sitting in the front seat. I explained how our family had grown in size and we chatted about her and CG, she told me she was officially an Old Lady, which I was very excited about as they suited each other well.

"Sugar?" I looked up to see Blade walking towards us.

"Sorry, I'm a bit early. The babies were falling asleep and I wanted to get them in the car, so I didn't disturb them later." He smiled at me, placed his hand on my cheek and kissed me. "You don't ever have to apologise or explain yourself to me.

Got it?" I nodded, he was talking quietly so no one else heard us. "Let's go." He looked at the car and back to me. "We need to get a bigger car." I laughed and agreed with him.

"You ride your bike, I don't know how long I am going to need to stay, and then you can at least still get back if you're needed here."

"I'm not leaving you there," he stated.

"Kade," I sighed.

"Fine, I'll follow behind you." I smiled, stood on my tip toes and gave him another kiss.

"Mummy!" Kelsey called out, I didn't break away from Blade.

"MUMMY!" She screamed even louder. We pulled apart and I looked at her through my open window in the car.

"Yes, sweetie?"

"I need to pee." I looked at Blade, he knew I didn't want to go back into that clubhouse. It held too many memories of me having to live there, having to dance, giving birth behind the bar, Cammie being taken and waking up one morning to find that Blade was gone.

"I'll take her," he mumbled. "Come on, sweetie." He pulled her out of her car seat and placed her on the floor. She ran around the side of the car and held onto my hand.

"I want mummy to take me." Blade looked at me and I gave him a little nod to say I would do it.

"Use the bathroom in my room."

"Ok."

Kelsey and I walked into the clubhouse and I was relieved to see that it was empty. No one was standing behind the bar, all the tables and chairs were empty and it was eerily quiet. We carried on walking until we reached Blade's room. I stopped as soon as we walked in, the bed was messy and it smelt like women's perfume. My stomach rolled at the thought of him being in here with other women, but I knew it was from the time he had Tiffany in there. He explained it all to me.

"Quick, Mummy." Kelsey moaned. Oh shit, I got caught up in

my thoughts. I hurried her into the bathroom and waited while she finished.

"Wash your hands." I lifted her up into my arms so she could reach the sink and washed her hands. "Let's get back to daddy." She nodded and we walked back towards the exit of the club. Just as we were about to walk out of the door Roxy stepped in front of us.

"Well, well. Who's this?" she asked, looking at Kelsey.

"I'm Kelsey," she said. I smiled politely and went to walk around her when she stepped in my path.

"Is this another way to trap him? With more kids?" she sneered.

"Kelsey, sweetie. Go to the car." I ran my hand over her brown curls and she skipped off out the door. Once she was out of sight, I looked back at Roxy who had her hands on her slim hips. She was wearing a tight mini skirt that was bright pink and a small black vest top that showed off her flat tummy, she had make-up plastered onto her face and too much perfume that made me want to gag at the smell of it.

"Where did you pluck a toddler from?"

"She's Kade's niece." I made a point of using his name, no one else was allowed to call him that apart from me.

"So you found another thing to trap him with? He doesn't want to be with you, he comes here and fucks me every night, more than once. He says my pussy is still nice and tight, not ruined by having a brat. Smell my perfume, I bet his room smells all of me."

"Oh and when was the last time he fucked you then?" I placed my hands on my hips waiting for her answer.

"Last night." I waved my hand out in front of me telling her to continue. "About ten o'clock," she smirked, clearly pleased with herself.

"Funny that, as at ten o'clock last night I was laid across his lap while he spanked me and fucked me hard and fast. Taking pleasure from my body. Not from some loose club whore."

She raised her hand and I braced myself waiting for her to hit me and when it didn't come I opened my eyes to see that Blade had her arm in his hand.

"You *do not* speak to an Old Lady that way and certainly don't threaten them with violence. She comes above you, learn the rules or get the fuck out!"

I was an Old Lady and there were rules to follow, but I didn't participate in the club lifestyle at the minute. I was wearing my leather cut, Blade expected me to especially when we were heading into another MC. She backed away from us and ran in the direction of their communal sleeping area.

"Come on, sugar. Let's get going." He grabbed hold of my hand and I didn't move. "You don't believe her, do you?"

"No, of course not. Your room does smell like her though. I think her plan was to get you into trouble with me." I moved closer to him and placed my hands on his hips.

"Bloody club whores are a pain in the fucking ass," he growled.

"Let's get out of here." I offered him my lips for a kiss and he didn't disappoint me. He claimed my mouth that made my knees weak and my underwear wet. I loved this man.

***

I pulled up in front of the Cornish Crusaders clubhouse and Cammie was sitting on the bench outside with Mason. She was straddling his lap, her long blonde hair falling down her back blew in the slight breeze. She was wearing her leather cut and she looked happy. I got out of the car and slammed the door shut, she looked over her shoulder and her face lit up when she saw it was me standing there. She jumped off of Mason's lap and ran over towards me. I held open my arms and we stood hugging each other for ages. We had been through a lot together. Without her, I would never have got through my time at the Destroyers clubhouse.

"I missed you," I told her.

"Missed you too. Where's my handsome boy?" She pulled back and opened the back door. "There he is. Hi, handsome," she cooed at him. She was rewarded with big smiles and flapping arms and legs that showed he was happy.

"Don't I get one of those?" Mason asked as he held his arms open for me. I didn't hesitate in walking towards him and wrapped my arms around his waist. He smelt of lime shower wash and I could hear his heart beating loudly as my head was pressed against his chest.

"VP." Blade greeted him.

"Blade, good to see you, man." He held his hand out and Blade shook it.

"Think I can have my woman back now?" I smiled and pulled away from Mason and stood in front of Blade watching Cammie with Liam. The girls were still asleep, we didn't get far before Kelsey was fast asleep in the front of the car. Blade placed his hands on my hips in a possessive way, showing Mason that I was his.

"Well, she was mine first." Mason chuckled.

"Mason!" I scolded him.

"Well, she loves me." Blade told him and I felt like I was back in the playground with children under the age of six.

"She loved me too." Mason shot back at him and I felt Blade's hands tighten on me.

"Sorry to tell you, Mason, but I have never loved anyone like I do Kade." Blade released his death grip on me and slipped his hands around my waist and pecked kisses down my neck. I giggled as it tickled. "Where's Daisy?" I asked Cammie, who now had Liam on her hip and was tickling him. He let out a little excited scream and we all laughed along with him.

"She's in her room. She didn't get home until a couple of hours ago." I shook my head, sighing with resignation.

"You go, sugar. I'll get the girls out." I kissed him quickly on the lips and headed into the clubhouse. There were a few of the guys around, eating.

"Hey, sweetheart. Good to see you." Solar smiled as he walked towards me. I reached up and gave him a quick hug. "How you been?" I pulled away from him and looked into his eyes. He looked tired.

"Yeah, good. What are you doing here?"

"I've come to see Daisy." I pointed over my shoulder towards her bedroom.

"Ah, yes. She's been different lately."

"Different how?"

"Moodier, out all hours. I'm worried she may get kicked out. She doesn't do a lot around here much anymore."

"Oh. I better go and see if I can find out what's bothering her." He nodded, turned around and walked away. His jeans hanging low on his hips, his biker boot laces dragging on the floor as he walked.

"Knock, knock," I called out as I pushed Daisy's door open. My mouth hung open at the state of the place. There was clothes scattered over the floor, empty drink bottles laying around and dirty plates piled up on her dressing table. She was laying faced down in her bed, blonde hair scattered across the pillow and a leg sticking out under the duvet. I walked towards the window and pulled open the curtains and pushed the window open, this room needed fresh air. I started cleaning up her room, figuring that the noise would wake her up.

"What the hell?" she moaned and turned over in bed. She locked eyes with me. "What are you doing here?"

"I came to see you. How are you?" I threw the empty beer bottles into a bin, she flinched at the noise. I'm guessing she had one hell of a hangover. I sat on the edge of her bed. "So? How are you?"

"Fine." She pulled herself up to lean against the headboard and she stared at me. "What?"

"You're not fine. What have you been up to? Where have you

been going?"

"Oh, so that's why you're here? The VP's Old Lady called you."

"Cammie was concerned for you. Where have you been going every night?"

"It's none of your business." She threw the covers off and climbed out of bed and stumbled to the bathroom, tripping over clothes and shoes. I waited until she was done. "You still here?"

"I'm not going anywhere."

"You soon will, when your family needs you." She riffled through her drawers until she found a pair of jogging bottoms and a hoody, she slipped her feet into some flip flops and opened her bedroom door.

"You're my family." She scoffed at what I said and walked out of the room. I followed her into the bar area and she stopped dead in her tracks when she saw Blade with Tegan and Cammie with Liam.

"Of course, you had to bring them with you," she said pointing at the kids. "Parading them around in front of me. Showing me what I'll never have… Why do you always get everything you want and I get nothing."

"Everything I want?" I couldn't believe what she was saying to me. I got close to her, I didn't want everyone to hear us. "I never wanted my husband to be killed in front of me, I never wanted to be part of an MC. I never asked to have a hysterectomy at twenty six and I never wanted my sister to go off the rails."

"I lost my husband too!" she screamed, tears running down her face.

"I know," I softly spoke as I went to put my arms around her.

"No. I don't need you." She pushed me away. "I don't need anyone." I watched her head for the door and as I went to go after her Blade called out;

"Sugar? You ok?"

"Yeah, I need to follow her. I need to talk to her some more." I was looking between him and the door, I didn't want to lose her, I needed to find some way to help her.

"Let's take the bike." I looked over his shoulder at the kids. "Cammie and Ashlyn have got them." I nodded and we made our way quickly to his bike.

*****

"What is she doing?" I said aloud as we sat on Blade's bike watching Daisy sitting on a park bench. She hadn't moved for over half an hour. "I need to go talk to her." Blade started moving and I placed my hand on his arm. "I need to go alone."

"Ok, sugar. I'll be here waiting."

"You don't have to wait, Daisy has her car." I pointed towards the red Astra parked only a few spaces away from us.

"I'm waiting." I nodded, there was no use in arguing with him. I handed him my helmet and kissed him quickly. "Love you."

"Love you too." I walked away from him, down some steps and across the grass until I was sitting next to Daisy on the park bench.

"What do you want?" She sighed, looking out straight ahead of her as a woman walked past with two children.

"Talk to me."

"Ok, what do you wanna talk about?" She looked at me briefly before looking away again.

"Daisy..." She held her hand up to stop me talking. I looked around us and saw a young, blonde, pregnant woman walk by us. A little boy was playing on the slide and a couple of other children were running around chasing each other. It made me smile that one day that would be my kids. I turned back to talk to Daisy and she had disappeared. I looked all around and couldn't see her anywhere. I hurried back over to where Blade was.

"You ok, sugar?"

"Did you see where she went?" I panted, I was so unfit. I needed to add cardio training into my workouts as well as yoga. He shook his head. "I was just looking around and when I turned back she was gone."

"Let's get back to the kids." He passed me my helmet and I climbed on the bike behind him.

Chapter 23

Blade

Heather was feeling annoyed and frustrated, she came here to help Daisy, to talk to her and all she had done was shut her out. She would disappear early in the mornings and not come back until really late or sometimes not at all.

"I think it's time to go back home." Heather sighed, she sounded defeated. "She won't talk to me, she won't let me help. There's nothing more I can do." I pulled her in close to me, I enjoyed nothing more than having Heather pressed up against me in bed. My arm was underneath her neck and her head and hand were on my chest.

"Ok, sugar." I kissed the top of her head. "You stay there. I'll get their milk." I pointed towards the babies. She smiled, pulled the duvet up to her chin and closed her eyes.

I walked into the kitchen and Mason and Cammie were in there, Cammie was sitting at the breakfast bar while Mason was making coffee.

"Morning," I grumbled.

"Hi, how's Heather?" Cammie asked.

"Not great, we're heading home today. Daisy doesn't want to be helped and it's upsetting Heather being here."

"Oh, I was hoping you were going to stay longer. I miss you all," she pouted.

"Yeah, about that…" I measured the powder babies' milk and put it in the bottles while I was waiting for the kettle to boil. "How do you fancy coming back for a few days? Ashlyn too?"

"Oh, I would love that," she chirped, clasping her hands together. Mason turned around and looked at her. "Babe, you don't mind. Do you?"

"I'm not overly happy about it," he complained. I poured the hot water into the bottles. Cammie jumped off her stool and stood in front of Mason who was sipping on his coffee cup.

"It'll only be for a few days. Heather needs me."

"Fine, but Drake goes with you."

"We don't need a prospect with us, we'll have Blade," she dismissed it and I could see the fury building on VP's face.

"Cammie," he warned.

"Fine, ok... I'm going to tell Ashlyn, then I need to pack." She rushed over to the kitchen door and as she was about to leave I called out,

"Let's surprise Heather later." She nodded, blew VP a kiss and walked out of the room.

"Thanks, man," VP groaned at me.

"What?" The bottles were cooler now and the babies would probably be awake by now.

"I have to be separated from my girl now. Not happy."

"I'm sure your dick can cope for a couple of days," I chuckled as I walked towards the door with the bottles in one hand and a cup of coffee in the other.

"Don't think it can, man." He scratched his stubble with his hand.

"You've always got a hand." I winked and left him to his sulking.

***

We had the car loaded with the kids and bags and we were ready to leave.

"You ready, sugar?" I snaked my arms around her waist and kissed her cheek.

"You know I can't leave without saying goodbye to Cammie and Ashlyn. It's bad enough that Daisy isn't here." She pushed my arms off her and was about to walk back into the clubhouse when Cammie and Ashlyn came walking out pulling suitcases behind them.

"What's going on? You both going somewhere?" Heather looked confused.

"We're coming to stay for a few days." Cammie told her. Heather, Ashlyn and Cammie all screamed in excitement and the suitcases were forgotten about as they all hugged. Drake and I picked up their bags and placed them in the boot of Ashlyn's car.

"I can't believe you're coming to stay. It's going to be so much fun, we'll have girly nights, dvds, popcorn…"

"Pizza for me." Drake said. Heather looked at him with her head tilted to the side.

"Drake has to come," Cammie stared saying. "Mason wasn't happy about me leaving." She looked over her shoulder and winked at the VP.

"Cammie, get that sexy ass over here!" he shouted, she slowly walked towards him and she squealed when he grabbed her by the waist and claimed her mouth.

"Come on, sugar. Get in." I held the door open for her and she stood by the car looking at me.

"You arranged this, didn't you?"

"Of course." I held her hand and wrapped it around my neck. I grabbed hold of her hips and lifted her until she was sitting on the bonnet of the car. She looked sexy as hell in her cut off shorts, sandals and vest top, her brown wavy hair was flowing over her shoulders. I stepped in between her legs, closer to her body and rained kisses all over her face, she let out a happy giggle and I was always satisfied knowing that I could make her happy.

"Ok, everyone. Let's go!" I called out. I pulled Heather off the car, kissed her and she climbed in and started the engine. VP was reluctant to let Cammie go but after she whispered something to him, his face lit up and he kissed her once more. He was definitely pussy whipped.

I took off down the road, followed by Heather, then Ashlyn's car and Drake kept close behind them. I was glad to be going home. I missed my bed.

Chapter 24

Blade

I walked into the clubhouse after being away for five days. It was quiet, the only person around was Roxy, who was behind the bar. I walked up to her.

"Where's everyone?"

"Church," she smiled at me.

"Fuck!" I swore, turned on my heel and headed to the church room. I didn't bother knocking, I just walked in. The room went quiet and all eyes were on me.

"Sorry, boss, didn't know we had a meeting." I sat in my usual chair and waited for him to carry on.

"Bump, I asked you to contact him." Prez said. I swung my gaze to Bump, who always sat in the back corner. His usually bushy beard was trimmed tidier today and he had a shirt on under his cut. Strange.

"Sent him a message, Prez." I pulled my phone out of my pocket and looked at the screen, no messages, no notifications, nothing.

"No messages received. Sorry, boss. Did I miss much?"

"We just started, it's been a slow couple of days. Agenda one, we have a large stag party at Skins tomorrow night. Privately booked the entire club, I'm gonna need at least four of you down there. Sort it out among yourselves. Agenda two, I've heard word that the Satan MC are back up and running, CG see what you can find out. Thought we killed all the fuckers. Agenda three, Blade, we got something for you. Meet me and VP out the front in ten minutes." He slammed the gavel down and we all disappeared out of the room.

I walked straight to the bar. "Whiskey," I demanded. Roxy made quick work of it and I downed the whiskey in one and made my way outside to wait for the Prez and VP. Were they finally letting me in on their secret? I felt happier knowing that I might have some concrete information for the police soon. I didn't want to run out of time and risk being separated from Heather and the kids.

I was leaning against my bike when Prez and VP strolled out. I stood up straighter, waiting to hear my instructions.

"Follow us." Prez said as he climbed on his bike and took off down the road, VP followed him and I fell in line with the pair of them.

We had been riding for about twenty minutes, I wasn't sure where we were headed and all the roads looked the same. Trees lined loads of the roads in Devon. Prez pulled up in front of what looked like an abandoned cottage surrounded by fields. I parked my bike next to theirs and they nodded to follow them in. I looked around to see if I recognised where I was and to see if there were any people around. It was completely deserted and I didn't have a clue where we were. I walked in through the rickety old door, bending slightly so I didn't hit my head. Inside, the rooms were old, dusty and there was beams overhead. It was empty inside and I walked into the room straight ahead, there was an old unused fireplace and a table and chairs. Prez was sitting at the table and VP had his back to me. As I walked closer, VP turned around and punched me in the face, I was dazed as I didn't expect that. Once I could focus he hit me again, this time knocking me off my feet. VP bent down grabbed the front of my cut and pulled me until I was sitting in a chair, my head rolled to the side. He stripped my cut off me.

"You don't deserve to wear this." VP spat in my face. I closed my eyes and once the dizziness stopped, I straightened my head and opened my eyes. Prez and VP were both standing in front of me with their guns out.

"What the hell is going on?" I asked, I went to pull my hands up to run them over my face and I realised my hands were tied behind my back to the chair.

"That's exactly what we want to ask you." Prez snarled. "You look confused, let me clarify. We got followed by the police, luckily after the shipment was delivered, then you disappear for five days when we announce we have a rat among us. Nothing fishy has happened since you've been gone."

"You think I'm the rat? I didn't even know about the drug shipment," I yelled, which earnt me another punch to the face, I could already taste blood coming off my split lip.

"Who you working for Blade?" Prez yelled as he paced the small room in front of me.

"No one. I'm a Devon Destroyer patched member, we don't rat on our own. We live and breathe for the club. We die for the club, we don't rat. This has been drummed in to me."

"What about those Cornish Crusaders?" VP asked.

"What about them?" I looked around for an escape route, there looked like there was a back door in the corner of the room, this place was old so I reckon with a bit of force I could kick it in, that would only work if I could get my hands untied and they left me alone.

"You've been with them quite a bit recently." Prez stated.

"I don't talk club business, I was there for my Old Lady these past few days."

"So, who you working for?" Prez asked.

"I work for the Devon Destroyers." VP came at me and I took a hit to the stomach, I gasped as it took my breath away, a hot sensation erupted through my body and I had to fight not to throw up.

"Let me ask again, who are you working for?"

"You, Prez." VP came at me again this time kicking me in the chest, causing my chair to fall over and smash as it was so rickety. My hands loosened and I pulled them out, I looked up and Prez and VP were both standing in front of me pointing their guns straight at my head. I put my hands up in surrender. I could feel blood trickling down the side of my head.

"I swear to you, I am no rat. I didn't know anything about a drug run. If you remember, I've only been back with the club a few short weeks. I get told jack shit." I used the bottom of my t-shirt to wipe the blood off the side of my face. It was no use, I think I need stitches.

"If we find out that it was you, not only will you die, but you will sit and watch while I torture and kill your whole family."

"Well then we haven't got a problem as it wasn't me," I stated. I saw the Prez nod subtly at VP and all I see is a boot coming my way.

***

I stumbled into my house a few hours later, all the lights were off and I tried to be quiet. I needed some water and aspirin for this blinding headache I had. I swore as I tripped over a kids' toy and fell into the kitchen worktop.

"Blade?" I turned around and saw Drake standing there. Shit, I forgot he was staying here and sleeping on the sofa. "You ok, man?" He turned the kitchen light on and I winced at the brightness. I must have passed out when I saw VP's boot coming for me. They did me over good, I had pain shooting through my back, in my neck, head and stomach.

"Shit," he swore coming closer. "Sit down." He pulled out a kitchen chair and pushed me to sit down.

"I'm ok, I just need some aspirin."

"Your eyebrow is bleeding," he said as he passed me a kitchen towel to press against it. "I'm gonna go get Heather."

"No!" I stood up and winced at how much it hurt. "I don't want her to know."

"She's gonna know, man. You won't heal overnight." He placed a glass of water and aspirin on the table in front of me and I sat down again slowly. "Who did this?"

"Prez and VP."

"Holy shit, man. Why?" He leant his hip against the counter and crossed his arms over his chest.

"They think I ratted."

"Well, didn't you?"

"Not yet. I don't have any information for the police."

"Kade? Drake?" I heard Heather's voice and slammed my hand down on the table in frustration when I tried to turn around. Pain shot all through my body and I didn't want to cry out.

"Come on in, sugar." I knew the moment she was standing in front of me as I heard her gasp. She fell to her knees and cupped my face in her hands. I screwed my face up in pain. "What the hell happened?"

"Club business," Drake and I said at the same time.

"Let me see." She pulled the towel away from my head. "We need to get you to the hospital, you need stitches. Let me just grab some clothes." I grabbed her hand before she disappeared.

"No hospitals."

"You need stitches. You could have broken ribs or anything."

"Get Ashlyn, she can fix my head, she's had nurse training. Everything else will heal, it'll just take time."

"Drake, can you…" Heather began.

"Sure, I'll go and wake her," he wandered off out of the room and Heather started rummaging around in the cupboards.

"Sugar, what are you doing?"

"Looking for a first aid kit. Oh, I found it." She knew not to ask me anymore questions about what happened and I was glad that she hadn't.

"Alright, alright. I'm moving." I heard Ashlyn, I looked over my shoulder and she walked in looking like a zombie, her eyes were still half closed, her hair was a mess and she was barely moving her feet. "Shit," she swore looking over at me, shaking her head. It wasn't the first time she had to patch me up and it wouldn't be the last.

"Here's the first aid kit." Heather said, placing it on the table beside me.

"I need coffee," she moaned, rubbing the sleep out of her eyes.

"I'll get it." Drake said as he moved through the kitchen, gathering coffee cups and filling the kettle with water.

"We need to check your ribs." Ashlyn said as she pushed my cut off my shoulders. "Arms up." I winced as I tried to lift my arms so she could pull my t-shirt off.

"Here, let me." Heather stepped forward and cut a line down the front of my t-shirt so it was easier to remove.

"Shit, woman, that's one of my favourite t-shirts," I complained.

"I don't care." I watched her as she took in my body, I had bruises covering my stomach, sides and lower back. Ashlyn very carefully examined me, pushing and prodding at my body.

"It doesn't look like they're broken, just badly bruised."

"Here, babe." Drake placed a coffee cup in front of Ashlyn and she smiled up at him.

"Thanks," she said shyly. I looked at Heather and back to Drake and Ashlyn and back to Heather again and she shrugged her shoulders at my silent question. Were these two a couple? If they were, Drake had better hope that Prez didn't find out, else he would be kicked out. A prospect isn't allowed to touch club women, Ashlyn wasn't one of the club whores but she was still being looked after and protected by the Cornish Crusaders.

"Let's stitch that eye up, I don't have anything I can give you for the pain."

"It feels numb anyway. Just go for it."

I sat there as still as possible while Ashlyn worked on my cut, Heather and Drake looked on quietly. I was ready for my bed. I also needed to decide what my next move was going to be, do I stop all the snooping and go to jail? Do I carry on and risk the life of my family? I didn't even know what shit they had on me, how long in jail I would be facing. I sighed as I struggled to figure out what was best to do. If I was being sent down then I needed to make sure Heather and the kids would be safe, they would need to go back to the Cornish Crusaders clubhouse. I needed to talk to Prez and see if he and the club would protect them, just in case. I wasn't a quitter and I would continue to fight.

Chapter 25

Heather

Blade had been home resting for a week. Cammie, Ashlyn and Drake were still here as Blade couldn't help much with the kids, so they offered to stay and help.

I walked into the living room after putting the babies and Kelsey to bed, Blade and Drake were slouched at opposite ends of the sofa, beer in hand. Ashlyn was sitting on the floor in front of Drake and she was leaning against his legs as she read her kindle. He was playing with her blonde hair that had fallen between his knees. I could hear Cammie on her phone, I looked over my shoulder and she was looking out the patio door whilst twirling some of her hair around her finger. I'm guessing she was on the phone to Mason. He wasn't too pleased when she told him that she was staying longer, he had threatened to come and get her to take her home and her answer was something along the lines of 'if your dick ever wants to see action again, you'll stay where you are'. Mason definitely had his work cut out for him with Cammie, she wasn't one to be bossed around, but she knew the rules of the club and she never disrespected him in front of the other members.

"Ok, girls night," I announced. "We've got facials, grease, dirty dancing, twilight, popcorn and I'm making cocktails."

"Oh, can we have sex on the beach?" Ashlyn asked, placing her kindle down on the coffee table and getting to her feet.

"Absolutely," I smiled as I walked into the kitchen to gather all the ingredients.

"What we doing?" Cammie asked as she sat on the stool at the breakfast bar, resting her chin in her hand.

"Making cocktails for our girly night then you should go home tomorrow," I told her.

"Really? Why?" Cammie looked confused.

"You miss him, he misses you. I'll be ok," I walked around the counter and pulled Cammie in for a hug. "I'll miss you though."

"I'll miss you too." Cammie squeezed me tighter.

"What's going on in here?" Blade asked, walking over to the bin and throwing his empty beer bottle away.

"They're going home tomorrow," I told him.

"We are?" Drake asked, leaning on the door frame. He filled most of it with his large size.

"I wanted to take Heather out tomorrow morning, can you wait until the afternoon?" Blade asked, looking at Cammie.

"Sure," she smiled. "I'm not going to tell Mase, I'm going to surprise him."

"On that note, we're out of here." Blade walked closer and pulled me into his arms.

"Where you going?" I gently placed my arms around his waist. He claimed that he was feeling better now and that he could resume all activities but I saw the pain on his face if he tried to lift Kelsey up or she threw herself at him.

"Got a bit of business to attend to. I'm gonna leave you to your girls night. Drake, you wanna join me?"

"Defo." He rubbed his hand over his stubbly jaw and Ashlyn looked over her shoulder at him and smiled. He nodded his head slightly and backed out of the room.

"I love you, sugar."

"Love you too. Be safe." Blade hadn't been out on his bike since his accident and I wasn't convinced he should be on it now, but I couldn't tell him that. It would only make him more determined to prove me wrong.

"I'll put the DVD in!" Ashlyn called out as she hurried into the living room, I grabbed the jug of sex on the beach and three glasses. Cammie and I laughed as we walked in the living room to find Ashlyn singing along to the Grease theme song. "What? I love this film."

We all settled down and started watching the film as we sipped on our cocktails, we had faces full of facial cream and we sang and danced along to the songs on the film.

"Look at me I'm Sandra Dee..." I started.

"Lousy with virginity..." Cammie continued.

"Won't go to bed til I'm legally wed..." Ashlyn sung. We all fell about laughing, this was the most fun I've had in ages. I never had a lot of girlfriends growing up, I found them all to be too bitchy. But I was definitely glad that I had met Cammie and Ashlyn, though the circumstances could have been better.

"So..." I started, looking at Ashlyn. "What's going on with you and Drake?" I had been dying to ask this all week, since I saw the exchange between them the night Blade came home hurt and bloody. But I had never got a moment alone with her.

"Nothing." She finished off her drink and stood up. We had all changed into our PJ's. Ashlyn was wearing tiny pale pink shorts and a matching t-shirt, her long blonde hair falling down her back. "I'm making more cocktails." She wandered off into the kitchen and Cammie gave me a look and a head nod. We both stood up and followed her in, we leant against the breakfast bar and stared at her. "What?" she placed her hands on her hips and stared at us.

"You're avoiding, answer the question." Cammie told her.

"Fine, there is nothing going on. He doesn't want me." She looked down at her hands and fiddled with her rings.

"Why do you say that?" Cammie and I got comfy on the stools as Ashlyn poured spirits and juices into a large jug.

"We kissed at one of the parties a few weeks ago and since then, nothing."

"It's not nothing. He hasn't kept his hands off you all week. I've seen the little touches here and there," I explained, taking a sip from the glass she placed in front of me. "Mmm, this is nice."

"I like it with more pineapple juice." Ashlyn stated as she took a sip and nodded in agreement with me that it tasted good.

"Do you know the club rule about prospects?" Cammie asked us. We both shook our heads. "They are not allowed to get involved with club women."

"She's not a club whore…"

"No, she isn't. But the Cornish Crusaders protect her so, therefore they see her as their property and until Drake patches in he is not allowed to touch her."

"What if he does?" Ashlyn asked, leaning on the kitchen counter so she could hear us better.

"He'll get kicked out."

"Oh." Ashlyn looked and sounded disappointed. "It's probably for the best anyway."

"What do you mean by that?" Cammie asked her.

"I'm too complicated to be with, I'm scared. What happened to me at that club…" She trailed off and I saw Cammie shiver out of the corner of my eye. We didn't want the conversation to turn this way.

"He should be patched in soon, right?" I asked looking between Cammie and Ashlyn.

"Soon, I think. It's normally after about a year." Cammie informed us.

"Oh, quick. Love this song!" Ashlyn called out as she went running into the front room. We walked in to see her doing the moves and singing 'Go Grease Lightning'. She looked happy and care free, we joined in and proceeded to sing along to the rest of the film.

***

Blade

"Where are we, man?" Drake asked as we pulled our bikes up to a wooded area.

"Cornwall," I answered, looking around us and making sure we wasn't followed.

"Shit, should we be that far away from the girls?"

"We won't be long, I just need to check on something." We were back at the warehouse where I saw Prez and VP. I needed some solid proof that would put them away for good. I wasn't in any shape to be fighting my way in, but I wanted to scope out the place some more. I wanted to know where all the entrances and exits were and how many men were around. I explained this all to Drake and he agreed to help me out. We stashed the bikes and made our way down the muddy, dusty hill. It was spookily quiet and that made me more on edge. I kept my movements light and my eyes were like a hawks, frantically looking around. I stopped when I could see the building. There were no lights on and no guards out the front. In fact, it looked deserted. We kept in the shadows in case we were being watched.

"I think it's empty, man." Drake whispered.

"I'm going for that window, to see if anyone is inside. Cover me, you got your piece?" He pulled his gun out of his jacket and released the safety. I nodded and made my way down the rest of the hill as quietly as I could. Once I reached the window, I listened, it was deadly quiet. I slowly peered into the window and it was in fact empty, no women, no mattresses, no Gloria and no VP or Prez. Fuck, I can't believe I missed an opportunity to get the info the police needed. I had a chance to put them away and I missed it. This could cost me my future with my family.

"Fuck!" I yelled as I slammed my fist into the wall. I heard movement behind me, I pulled my gun out and aimed it as I spun around. I breathed a sigh of relief and dropped it as soon as I saw it was Drake. "It's empty."

"Let's get out of here." I nodded in agreement and we made the quick walk back to our bikes.

"I need a drink, we passed a bar on the way in." I climbed onto my bike and we made our way to the bar.

We pulled up to the 'Queen's Inn' it didn't look like the normal place we would visit but I was pissed off and needed a drink or two. We parked our bikes by the side of the building and headed inside. From the outside, you looked like you were walking into a country pub, but inside it was dark; a few scattered tables, a long bar, a stage and a dance floor. This was not what I was expecting. We walked up to the bar and I ordered two whiskeys. I pushed one towards Drake and he downed it in one. I looked around and there was a group of women at a corner booth, drinking and laughing without a care in the world.

"Give me another," I demanded to the barman. He looked at Drake and he shook his head, indicating that he didn't want one. I noticed that one of the women kept looking our way, she had long straight black hair, a black corset, black shorts and fish net stockings, finishing off by a pair of black killer heels.

"What you doing, man?" Drake asked, stepping in front of me and blocking my view.

"Nothing." I slung back my drink and nodded for another one. "You being a pussy and not drinking?"

"One of us has to be able to get us home tonight."

"Hey, handsome. You wanna dance?" The woman I had been watching came over and had her hand on my thigh. I smiled back to her, grabbed her hand and started to stand up.

"What the fuck, man?" Drake growled, pushing me back into my seat.

"What?"

"You really going to do this?" He pointed to the woman.

"Why not? I've fucked up my life now, I may as well screw it up a bit more." I stood up and wrapped my hand around her back. "What's your name, sweetheart?"

"Heather." She smiled, turning her body in closer to mine, that was when reality hit me. Shit, what was I doing? What was I thinking?

"He's not interested." Drake told her, pushing her away from me.

"I saw the way he was looking at me, he wants me. I'm not going anywhere."

"Fuck off!" Drake shouted in her face, she paled and scurried away. "Let's get out of here." He threw some money on the bar and grabbed me by my arm, leading me out of the bar. We walked around the corner of the pub to where we parked our bikes, he pushed me up against the wall and threw a punch, hitting me square on the jaw causing my head to jolt. "What the fuck were you thinking? You have a gorgeous, kind and amazing Old Lady at home, looking after *your* three kids. You were gonna throw that away for some slut." He paced in front of me and I rubbed my hand over where he had hit me. It was a good solid punch, he was built like a brick house.

"You get one punch for free. Anymore and I take your ass down," I warned him, he stopped pacing and looked at me laughing.

"You ok to ride? Or do we need to come back and get your bike tomorrow?"

"I can ride." I straddled my beloved bike, I wasn't leaving it anywhere. Drake followed behind me and we made our way back home.

Chapter 26

Heather

"Where are we going?" I asked Blade as I climbed on the back of his bike. We had planned to go out this morning, but Tegan was being fussy, but after her lunch time nap she was much happier.

"It's a surprise." He grabbed the side of my thighs and pulled me closer to him. "Wrap your arms around me."

"I don't want to hurt you."

"And I don't want you to fall off." I wrapped my arms around him, trying not to hold on too tight. "Sugar, tighter." I held on tighter else we were never going to get anywhere. Once he was satisfied, he started the bike and we sped off down the road. This was the only the second time I had left all three children and I felt a little apprehensive about it. I knew I could trust Cammie and Ashlyn and knew that Drake would keep them all safe.

We travelled for about twenty minutes, when I felt Blade slowing down I looked around and noticed that we were at the beach. He knew this was one of my favourite places to be. As we were going slowly around the car park, I pulled my helmet off and shook my hair out, I loved feeling my hair blowing around in the breeze. Blade pulled in up high by the cliffs, the view was outstanding. I climbed off the bike and walked over to a bench. Blade followed me.

"I love it here, thank you." I kissed him quickly, not wanting to take my eyes off the view. Far out on the horizon, the sea was bright blue and settled and as it go closer to shore it crashed on the rocks, creating bubbles and foam. The sound was calming and it was one of the places I could sit and relax all day even in the rain.

"I love you, sugar."

"I love you too."

He turned his body towards mine and held my hands in his. "I never knew it was possible to love someone as much as I love you, to want to protect you, keep you safe and love you all day long, every day. You, Liam, Kelsey and Tegan are my world and I would be completely lost without all of you," he paused as he rummaged around inside his jacket. I watched as he pulled out a ring box and held it in front of me, closed. "I know we can't get married, because technically you are still married to James and I'm married to Willow..." He took another deep breath, I knew it wasn't possible for us to get married as our other halves were cleaned up and buried, no funerals, no evidence of their deaths. As far as anyone knew, they were still alive.

"I want you to have this ring and be mine, forever. What do you say? Always together forever?"

"Oh, Kade. Yes, of course I will always be yours. Isn't that what this means?" I asked pulling at my leather cut.

"It is, but I hated seeing that finger on your left hand bare." He opened the box and settled inside was two rings, matching wedding rings. One for me and one for him. "Heather, I give you this ring to show you how much I love you, respect you and cherish you. I will always protect you and our family. I love you." He pushed the ring on my finger and I gazed at it. It was a white gold Celtic ring, the delicate pattern on it was amazing. I pulled out the other matching ring from the box and placed it on Blade's finger.

"Kade, I give you this ring to show you how much I love you, respect you and cherish you. I will always keep our family safe, happy and healthy. I love you so much." A tear ran down my face and Blade wiped it away as he cradled my face in his large hands, his soft lips and stubble caressing my skin, first a kiss on my cheek, my lips and my neck.

"Mmm," I moaned in pleasure. His lips moved back to mine and he showed me how much he loved me with a soft and passionate kiss that lit my body on fire. I hoped that feeling would never end, that he would always have this effect on me. Once we separated he pulled me onto his lap, my back to his chest and we watched the sun setting. I didn't know how long we had been sitting there, we were interrupted by the sound of Blade's phone ringing. I jumped up quickly, panicking that there was a problem with the kids.

"Club." Blade told me as he looked at the caller display. I sat back down beside him as he answered it. "Yeah… Ok, yeah I'll be there in ten minutes." He sighed as he wrapped me in his arms again. "I need to stop by the clubhouse on the way home, it won't be for long." I nodded, I didn't want to leave the little bubble we were in but Blade was needed and it was never a good thing to keep the club waiting.

***

I didn't want to go into the clubhouse as Blade said he wouldn't be long. I had been sitting on a picnic bench outside for nearly an hour and it was starting to get unnervingly dark. I needed the toilet too, so I got up and walked inside. The club was busy, girls were dancing on the stage, the bar was busy and it was noisy. I didn't want anyone to see me so I quickly hurried to Blade's room to use the toilet. I didn't want to have to walk past the bar to get to those toilets. Once I was finished, I washed my hands and went in search for Blade. As I walked down the hall I heard some voices in the Prez's office, the door was ajar so I peeked through the gap. The Prez and VP were standing there talking, no Blade. I went to walk away when I heard the words Satan MC. I stood back from the door so they couldn't see me and listened.

"I don't know what the fuck happened, boss. No one knows

we are working with the Satan MC. No one knows about the merge." I gasped at what I was hearing. Shit, did they hear me? I peeked back into the room and saw two sets of eyes staring at me.

"Get her, keep her quiet." Prez ordered. I ran away as fast as my legs could take me, I looked behind and saw Ripped gaining on me. I ran straight for the exit, praying that Blade was outside waiting for me, I was relieved to see that he was. I looked behind again and saw that Roxy had stopped Ripped, I needed to thank her for that one day.

"Sugar?" Blade looked worried.

"Get on the bike, quick, we gotta go." Blade climbed on the bike and sped off even before I had a chance to put my helmet on.

"Helmet," he shouted to me. I nodded and slipped it over my head. "What happened?" he asked. We had speakers in our helmets so we can talk to each other.

"Just get me home," I shouted.

"Sugar, you need to tell me what happened." I felt the bike slowing down before Blade pulled into a layby.

"No, don't stop, why are you stopping?" I slapped at his back.

"Talk to me," he turned around the best he could and flipped open the visor on my helmet.

"I heard Prez and VP talking. I was looking for you. They mentioned working for the Satan MC and a merge."

"Fuck!" he roared. "We gotta get you out of here." He slammed my visor down, slipped his helmet back on and then we were flying down the dual carriageway.

"Where are you going?" I panicked, home was in the other direction.

"We need to get you away from them. We have to put distance between us and fast. Before they find us."

"What do you mean? I want to go home."

"We can't go home, sugar."

"Kade, our children are there," I sobbed. "Stop the bike."

"No."

"Stop the bike." I hit his back. "Stop the bike." I hit him again. "Stop the bike." My head fell against his back and I cried.

Blade

I felt the pain shooting through my chest at the turmoil Heather was going through. I didn't want to keep her away from our kids, but I couldn't let her go back there either. She heard private information and I couldn't risk letting them get to her, not only would they kill her, they would enjoy it. They would probably rape her and torture her, enjoying every moment of it. I would never let them hurt her like that.

"Kade, please," she sobbed. We had been travelling for over two hours, I was vigilant in checking my mirrors and was convinced no one was following us. I pulled in to the car park of a Travelodge to see if they had any rooms for the night.

"Come on, sugar." I tapped her leg and she climbed off the bike, pulling her helmet off. Her eyes were red and puffy. I pulled her in closer to my chest and she broke down.

"Please, Kade, let's go back. I can't leave our children, I just can't, please," she begged.

"They will be fine with Cammie, Ashlyn and Drake. Let's get a room and then we can phone them." She nodded, I grabbed her hand and led her into the entrance.

The reception was clean, tidy and minimalistic. Sat behind the desk was an older woman, with short dark hair.

"Do you have any rooms available, please?" I asked.

"For how many nights?"

"Just one." She kept looking over at Heather who was still sobbing.

"Yes." I handed over my credit card, I didn't care how much it would cost, I just needed a place where we could lay low and rest. As she processed the transaction she looked at Heather again.

"Miss, are you ok?" She handed over a box of tissues and Heather took a couple, dabbing at her eyes.

"Yes," she sniffed. The woman looked from me and back to Heather.

"If you don't want to go with this man, I can call the police," she informed her, now standing up. She placed my credit card back in front of me.

"Oh, no. He's my husband, we've just had some bad news, that's all. Thank you for your concern though." She nodded her head. "He may look rough around the edges but he is a teddy bear really." She smiled.

"As long as you're sure."

"Yes. Thank you, it's good that you checked."

"Ok. Your room is on the third floor. Take the door at the end of the corridor, up the steps and it's the fourth door on your left." She handed me the room key and we walked away from her.

As soon as we walked in the room, Heather turned to me.

"Give me your phone. I need to call Cammie."

"We need to use the hotel phone. I need to keep this one turned off in case it can be traced." She rushed to the hotel phone and called Cammie. "Let me talk to Drake when you're done." She nodded.

"Oh god, Cammie." Was all Heather said before she started sobbing again, she couldn't talk so I grabbed the phone.

"Hey, Cammie. How's the kids?"

"They're all good. Just put them to bed. What time you coming back?"

"There has been a bit of a problem, I need to talk to Drake."

"Yeah ok. DRAKE!" I pulled the phone away from my ear as she screamed down it. "It's Biade." I heard her tell him.

"Hey, man. What's up?"

I explained everything that Heather had heard and told him

we needed to stay away for a bit, I didn't tell him where we were. I couldn't run the risk of anyone finding us.

"I need you to take the girls and the kids back to your club. Get the Prez to call a lockdown, no one comes into that club. I'm trusting you with our children."

"Absolutely. We'll leave straight away."

"I'll call when I can. Thanks." I hung up the phone. Heather was laying on the bed curled up in a ball, crying. "Come on, sugar." I carried her over to the en-suite and sat her on the toilet seat while I switched the shower on and found the correct temperature. "You'll feel better after a shower." I pushed her leather cut off her shoulders and she looked up at me.

"Better? You think a shower is going to make me feel better? After we have just left our children? What if something happens to them?"

"It won't. Drake is taking everyone back to the Cornish Crusaders MC. They'll be safe there. I promise." I pulled her t-shirt over her head and unclipped her bra. Her breasts bounced free and I felt the swell of my cock. I held hold of her hand as I got her to stand up. I dropped to my knees, pulled off her ballet flat shoes and popped open the button on her jeans and dragged them down her legs, along with her pale pink underwear. Once she was standing in front of me, naked, I made quick work of my clothes, leaving them in a pile on the floor.

I pulled her into my chest as we stood underneath the small shower head, trying to keep water on both of us. She cried as I ran my hand up and down her back.

"Please, can we go back?"

"No."

"Please, Kade, don't keep me away from our babies."

"I said no." I didn't want to be firm with her, but if that was the only way she would listen than that was how I was going to have to be. I washed her body and hair all while she stood there motionless, she had given up doing anything, she was like a ghost of a person. After I scrubbed my body, I wrapped a towel around Heather and began drying her body while I dripped on the bath mat.

"You drying your hair?" I tightened the towel around her and secured it. She nodded as she walked out of the bathroom. I wrapped a towel around my waist and picked up our clothes off the floor. I grabbed our underwear, ran some water into the sink and cleaned them the best I could with the hand soap. Once they were cleaned, I ringed them out and placed them on the heated towel rail to dry. They should be dry by morning. After I dried myself completely, I walked out just as Heather had finished drying her hair. It was flowing around her shoulders in waves.

"Come on." I pulled her towards the bed and we both climbed in, minus the towels.

"Oh, Kade. I'm so sorry. I shouldn't have stayed and listened. This is all my fault." She climbed on top of me and buried her face in my neck, wrapping her arms around me. I soothed her with rubbing circles on her back. "You can leave me here and go back if you want."

"Hey." I pulled her away from my neck and grabbed her left hand. "You see this?" she nodded. "This means we're together, forever, always."

"Ok." I pulled her back down and she laid her head on my chest, she drew lazy circles on my chest and I felt her nipple bars against my chest every time she breathed. I couldn't stop my cock hardening, I had a naked Heather on top of me, any man would be hard. "I feel numb, I need to feel something more," she whispered as she manoeuvred herself so she was straddling my hips. She was hot, wet and needy and although the timing felt wrong to be doing this, I knew it was what she needed. She rose above me and I slipped inside of her. We groaned at the same time. She sat still adjusting to me and I ran my hands up her thighs, over her tummy and plucked and pulled at her nipple bars. I felt her tighten around me so I did it again. My hands slipped down her sides and to her ass, I tapped her gently telling her I needed her to move. She bent forward resting her hands by the side of my head, her hair causing a curtain around us. I moved my hips off the bed, thrusting into her and she cried out, closing her eyes. I placed my hand on the side of her neck, my thumb stroking the side of her cheek and I lowered her head to mine so I could kiss her. We moved together slowly and passionately, our kisses only pausing when we ran out of breath or to moan in pleasure.

"Kade," she whispered as I felt her convulsing around me. I slammed into her a couple more times and then my release shot into her. She slumped against me, exhausted no doubt from all the crying. I didn't want to move her, I wanted us close. I moved her hair out of my face and slowly closed my eyes hoping sleep would make things clearer in the morning.

Chapter 27

Blade

I didn't want to stay in one place for too long, there was always more chance of us being found if we didn't keep moving on. As Heather dressed, I picked up the hotel phone and made a call.

"Hello."

"Brett, its Blade."

"It's good to hear from you, thanks for the tip. We got them, just Prez and VP, all the rest of the boys come up clean."

"You arresting them?"

"Just as soon as we've been through all evidence from the crime scene."

"Crime scene?"

"Yeah, the one you called us about, we busted in. Saw all the women and Prez's wife tied to a chair. Arrested a couple men, made a deal with a couple of them." Who called them? I certainly didn't. Who else knew about it? Dad?

"They ratted?"

"Sure did."

"Who were they? Satan MC?"

"I can't offer out that information."

"How long until they're arrested?"

"Hopefully, no longer than a couple of days."

"That's great news." I hung up just as Heather walked back in the room.

"What's great news? Can we go home?" She looked hopeful.

"Not yet, sugar. The police will have Prez and VP arrested in a couple of days hopefully."

"The police?" She looked confused as she ran her hands through her hair attempting to tame it as we had no hair brush.

"Yeah." I stood off the bed, grabbed my phone that was still turned off and my wallet. "Let's get out of here." We walked out of the room and down the stairs hand in hand, I dropped the key card off at the desk and we climbed back on the bike.

"Can we go at least a bit closer to home? Just so we are closer in case our children need us, please?"

"Ok, sugar." We set off back down the dual carriageway. They would never expect us to still be in Cornwall, they would expect us to be long gone, so it would be the perfect place to hide.

After a few hours, we pulled up to a large supermarket for food and a change of clothes. We brought a back pack to put it all in so Heather could carry it on her back.

"Where are we?" Heather asked as I pulled in to a Premier Inn.

"Truro." We climbed off the bike and it was like de-ja-vu all over again, getting a room to hide out in. Once we were in the room, I unpacked our bag, handing Heather some food and water.

"Thanks."

"I also got you this." I handed her a large pocket knife.

"Why?"

"Just in case you need to protect yourself, please keep it on you. It just flips open like this." I showed her and made her show me she knew how to use it several times before I was happy. We settled on the bed and watched some TV.

"Can I call Cammie?"

"Sure, sugar. Get her to kiss the kids for me."

I ate a sandwich as I watched some game show shit on the TV while Heather talked to Cammie. She sounded happier knowing that the kids were ok and that we weren't too far away from them.

"Babe, Prez wants to talk to you." I grabbed the phone from her as I finished the last bite of my sandwich.

"Hello."

"Blade, just wanted you to know, we are on lockdown. We haven't heard anything from the Devon Destroyers and the kids are safe and happy."

"Thanks, Prez. I really appreciate your help. This should all be over soon."

"Yeah?" he asked. I explained what Brett had told me and he said he would get some contacts to keep their ears to the ground too.

***

We had been cooped up in that room for nearly twelve hours and I was getting restless. It was ten o'clock at night and dark. "You wanna go for a ride?" I asked Heather. She sat up from her laying position on the bed and nodded. "Great, grab your cut."

As we climbed on the bike she whispered;

"Are we safe?" I nodded.

"If for any reason we do get attacked, I want you to jump on my bike and get the hell away."

"I don't know how to ride." Shit, when this was all over it would be the first thing I'd teach her.

"I'll teach you. Helmet on." Once we were ready, I took off down the road, it was nice to be on my bike with Heather pressed against me. There was no feeling like it.

After we had been riding for thirty minutes, I kept checking my mirrors, I was sure we were being followed.

"What's wrong?" Heather asked.

"Nothing."

"Kade, don't keep things from me. Not now."

"I think we're being followed. Hold on." I didn't really know the roads around here, I tried to escape down a few side roads but the lights kept following us, in fact, they were gaining on us. I abruptly turned a corner and zoomed down a side alley. "Shit!" I roared.

"What?"

"Dead end." I turned the bike around and there were two bikes headed for us blocking off the entrance. "Shit, get off the bike." I looked around frantically. "Keep your helmet on for protection, hide in that corner by the bins and if anyone but me comes at you. Use that knife, sugar."

"I love you."

"Don't do that. We're going to be fine. We'll be going home to our babies. Ok?" She nodded and I pushed her towards the corner as I saw two figures heading towards us. I pulled my helmet off, I needed to talk to these guys.

As they got closer I saw that it was VP and Bump. I might have known Bump would be here, he always had a soft spot for Heather. I thought at first that it was her pregnancy, but even after Liam was born he was still after her.

"Give her up, Blade." VP shouted. I crossed my arms over my chest. "You know the club comes first, brother." Was he fucking kidding me?

We were stood in a stand-off position, who was going to draw a weapon first? I kept an eye on Bump, he was looking in the direction that Heather went and I knew I would have to fight off VP in order to save her.

"Hand her over, Blade." VP said again.

"No, she knows to keep quiet. She won't say anything."

"No way, she knows our plans. You're a fucking rat, who knows who you have told."

"He's the rat?" Bump asked. VP nodded and while they were distracted, I pulled out my gun and shot at VP. The bullet pierced his skin on his shoulder and he yelled out in pain. I aimed my gun at Bump and he fired shots at me, I dived to the floor and threw my knife. It got him high on his thigh. He looked at me, smirked and yelled;

"I'll have fun using this on your Old Lady." I saw movement out the corner of my eyes and Heather ran at Bump, he was startled and grabbed hold of her, they both fell to the ground, him landing on top of her, he let out a startled gasp, his eyes widening.

"Kade!" Heather yelled and the VP jumped up, gun in his hand. I didn't hesitate, I shot his hand and fired several more shots at his chest. He fell to the ground and I ran over to Heather. I pulled Bump off her and her knife was sticking out of his stomach.

"Oh god, what have I done?" She sobbed as she looked at him laying still, blood pooling around him.

"It was self-defence, it was either him or you. Got it?" She nodded. "Let's get out of here." I grabbed the knife out of Bump and wiped the blood off on his jeans. "We don't want to leave this evidence behind."

"What are we going to do about them?"

"I'll call the Crusaders and see if they can get a clean-up crew here." I dragged her back to the bike and once we were seated, I spun off out of the alley and headed back to the premier inn to sleep and then first thing in the morning we were heading for the Cornish Crusaders MC.

Chapter 28

Heather

Once we reached the Cornish Crusaders clubhouse, I didn't waste any time, as soon as the bike had come to a stop, I yanked my helmet off and ran at full speed in the door. I stopped dead in my tracks when I saw Kelsey sitting at a table colouring with Prez and Carla's kids. Her head snapped up when she heard a noise.

"Mummy!" she called out and came running towards me. I crouched down and caught her in my arms. I held her close to me and breathed in her scent.

"Hi, baby. Are you ok?"

"Yes, where have you been?" She pulled back to look at me.

"Just on a trip with daddy." She wriggled for me to put her down and I rushed in the room eager to see Liam and Tegan. Liam was sitting with Tat and Cammie was feeding Tegan. I went for Liam first. As he saw me coming, his arms and legs started flapping, I picked him up and blew raspberries on his neck, causing him to giggle. "Oh, I missed you sweet boy." I held him to my chest and rocked him back and forth. I walked over towards Cammie and looked down at my little girl. "Hi, sweet girl." I ran my finger over her cheek, she stopped sucking on her bottle and let out a cry. "Come here." Cammie placed her in my arms and I was happy that both my babies were safely in my arms. Tegan stopped crying and laid her head against my chest. I smiled at Cammie with thanks and she squeezed my hand in response, I knew I could always count on her for anything.

"Daddy!" Kelsey called out. I turned around as Blade picked

her up. I walked towards him and he shifted Kelsey onto his hip and held his arm open for me to join them. We were complete again, a family.

***

Blade

I didn't think I would ever be standing here again, yet here I was about to walk in the doors to the Devon Destroyers clubhouse. I took a deep breath and pushed the doors open, the bar area was quiet, no club whores around which was strange. I heard shouting coming from the room we had church in and headed that way.

Everyone stopped shouting and looked at me as I stood in the doorway.

"Well, well. Look who's here. Bring that whore of yours with you?" Prez asked.

"Shut it, Dad." CG said. "Is Heather ok?" he asked me. I nodded.

"Sit down, everyone." Prez instructed as he stayed standing. I looked around the room and saw a box sitting in the middle of the table.

"What's that?" I whispered to CG. He shrugged, I'm guessing he didn't know. Maybe this was what the Prez was about to tell us.

"As you all know, we have a rat amongst us... Someone found out a secret of mine and ratted to the police. Now that person is not leaving here alive. If I am going down, he is going down with me. Let me introduce you to the rat." Does he mean me? I technically never told the police anything, I assumed it was my dad.

"Blade, stand up." Prez instructed. My chair scraped back on the floor as I climbed to my feet. "This gentlemen is our rat."

He drew his gun and pointed it at me, I looked around the room at the stunned faces.

"Yeah, ok. I admit it, I was approached by the police, told to rat you out or I go to prison. I was not leaving my family here unprotected. But I didn't rat on you, someone else did. I saw you at your warehouse with the Satan MC and when I went back for more info it was empty."

"What's this about the Satan MC?" Itch asked.

"He was planning a merge with them," I informed the club.

"That is something that has to be voted on at church." Itch yelled.

"It was for the good of the club." Prez stated. "Anyway, this guy sold me out and my informants told me the police are coming for me. So you aren't living to see that." He cocked his gun and aimed it at me. The other guys around the table started yelling. All that kept flashing through my head was Heather, Kelsey, Liam and Tegan, I hoped they would be ok without me, I hoped that Heather would find someone else she could love and trust.

"You sold us out, Prez!" Riz yelled.

"We don't want to be involved with Satan shit!" Itch roared.

"Enough!" Prez screamed. "He dies, now!" I was preparing to have my life taken from me. I was saying a prayer that Heather and the kids would cope without me. I was praying that they would always be safe and happy.

"It was me!" CG yelled. Everyone fell silent. "It wasn't Blade, it was me. I have been working with the police. I hated the way this club was run, I hate being a member. I wanted it to stop, all of it."

"My own son sold me out." Prez said, lowering his gun and falling into his chair.

"You always favoured Ripped over me. You didn't play football with me, you taught me how to shoot a gun. I lost my virginity to a club whore. I hate this world, I don't want to be part of it. You needed to be stopped. You had my mum tied up to a chair in that warehouse doing God knows what to her." We were all stunned, yeah CG was quieter than the rest of us, but I never expected to find out that he was working with the police. If they had him why did they need me?

"So, Dad, I'm the rat, you going to shoot me?" he asked, placing his gun on the table, stretching his arms out to show he was no longer armed with a weapon.

"Get out," he said slowly and quietly. "While you still can."

"What's in the box?" I asked.

Prez looked at me, smirking. "The captain always goes down with his ship."

"Fuck, BOMB!" I yelled, yanking the door open in an attempt escape. As I scrambled out of the room I saw the club whores sitting around drinking. "EVERYBODY OUT!" We were all flying towards the exit, when I was lifted off the ground and my ear drums burst with the loud bang, glass was shattered everywhere, covering us. I turned my body over to see the clubhouse up in flames and bodies lying all over the ground. Some were moving and others weren't. I tried to get up to help, but my body objected, my eyes rolled to the back of my head and I passed out.

Epilogue

Blade

A year later

I was voted as the new Prez for the Devon Destroyers MC. I had chosen CG as my VP but he didn't want it. He left the club and took Tiffany with him.

I decided to break the rules and patched in Wayne and Dwayne straight away, they had both been prospects for under a year, but I trusted them completely. I also gave Wayne the VP spot, he had spent hours protecting Heather and Liam and this was the one guy I wanted at my side. Around the church table now, we had myself, Buzz (Wayne – due to the fact his hair was always clipped off short. After the bomb explosion he had to have surgery to remove some shrapnel from his head, he loves telling the story along with showing them the scar) Riz, Itch, Ice, (Dwayne – He was always ice cold, even in the heat of summer he would always be wrapped up in jumpers and jeans) Bear, (my old man, who was covered head to toe in thick brown hair) he had betrayed his club and was kicked out, we found him one evening dumped outside our gates with his club tattoo burnt from his skin, he was in bad shape. To this day, he still hasn't told me why he was kicked out, he said it was best that I didn't know. We voted and the majority favoured for him to join us so here he was sat around the table and also two new prospects, Dan and Fred.

The old clubhouse was blown up and there was no saving it so we now lived in the same area but in an old run down hotel. We spent the past year improving the state of it and I had the top floor converted into a place for me, Heather and the kids to live.

"Agenda one, our one year party of owning this shit hole is tonight, let's have fun. Agenda two I need some guys to escort the skins girls here for their show. It's going to be a good one. Agenda three, don't disrespect the girls and stop bringing in new club whores. There are plenty around here to keep you guys happy." I slammed the gavel down and the guys got up and left the room. I ran my hand over my face, I looked between my fingers when I heard the door open. I smiled when I saw my sexy Old Lady standing there with Liam on her hip.

"Hey, sugar."

"Dad, Dad, Dad, Dad." Liam called out, arms stretched out in front of him.

"Someone has been calling out for you all morning." She passed him over to me. Once he was in my lap, I pulled Heather close for a kiss. We only broke away when we heard a shrill scream.

"Tegan?" I asked. She nodded. "How was Kelsey at play group this morning?"

"She ran straight in, no backward glance at me, our little girl has grown up, I can't believe today is her first day at play group," she smiled. "I best see what Tegan has gotten herself into now. Love you."

"I love you, sugar."

I looked down at Liam, he had picked up the gavel and started hitting the table with it, giggling after every time he done it.

"One day, Son. This will all be yours, but let's keep that a secret between us for now. Mummy wouldn't be happy."

The End

Which book next?

Whose book would you like to read next?
Cammie & Mason
CG (Neil) & Tiffany
Ashlyn & Drake
Solar & ???

Drop me a little message on my wall on facebook telling me whose book you want to read next.

https://www.facebook.com/pages/Author-Kacey-Hamford/572126959568554

Want more of Blade? Head over to Amazon and check out The Last Betrayal (Crusaders MC #2) by L. Grubb where you can find out what he got up to when he left Heather. Due out December 2015.
While you wait check out book 1 in the Crusaders MC series – An honest mistake by L. Grubb

About the Author

Kacey Hamford is a pen name for me (Kelly). I am in my thirties and started this journey in 2014, I love to read romance books about rockstars, so thought I would have a go at writing one myself. I really enjoyed it and got a boost of confidence once my books started selling.

I have gone on to write a young adult series, set in a college. This series is still on going.

I also have an MC series, it was something different for me to write and I enjoyed it so much, especially when I got readers telling me they would love to read books about the sub characters.

I work full time as a dog groomer, I love to read and my friends and family are very important to me. They are all so supportive of my writing career and encourage me to carry on.

For information on upcoming books please go to:
https://www.facebook.com/pages/Author-Kacey-Hamford/572126959568554

Other book wrote by Kacey Hamford -
The Rocking Series:
Book 1. Rocking Esme
hyperurl.co/6p848k
Book 2. Rocking Scarlett
hyperurl.co/tjvgpx
Book 3 Rocking Marcy
hyperurl.co/ffymuj
Book 4 Rocking Ashton

hyperurl.co/9hrs7s
Book 5 Rocking Danni
hyperurl.co/tcitkv

<u>Chance Series</u>
Book 1 - Taking A Chance
Hyperurl.co/puqylu
Book 2 – Giving A Chance
hyperurl.co/h6tezv

<u>South Coast Brothers</u>
Book 1 – Devon Destroyers MC
mybook.to/DevonDestroyers

Printed in Great Britain
by Amazon